# LOST VALLEY

## John Hunter

# CHIVERS

**British Library Cataloguing in Publication Data available**

This Large Print edition published by BBC Audiobooks Ltd, Bath, 2009.
Published by arrangement with Golden West Literary Agency.

U.K. Hardcover ISBN 978 1 408 43256 3
U.K. Softcover   ISBN 978 1 408 43257 0

Printed and bound in Great Britain by CPI Antony Rowe, Chippenham
and Eastbourne

# CHAPTER ONE

It was in the Bill Williams country of northwestern Arizona, with the cold wind howling down the mountain, that Dave Harden met the old Mexican and found that bread cast on the water really did come back swelled a thousandfold, but it took him a while to learn that the return did not necessarily have the same substance to it.

It was early spring and it was cold. Dave was working the day shift at the McCracken Mine. The late afternoon whistle blew and Harden joined the crew coming off shift as they walked the mile into town, but he did not stop with them as they swarmed into the saloon.

Sweating from eight hours of swinging the single jack and chilled through by the wind off the snow on the eastern mountains around the big canyon, he would have appreciated a drink. He liked a cup of liquor as well as the next man. But Dave was saving his money.

Summertimes, Dave was a prospector, one of a breed of young and hardy men who spread out over the wide, empty land in great numbers yet, because of its vastness, seldom ran across one another. They had to be young and hardy, and knowledgeable and tough, to hunt ore through the Arizona hills in the early seventies. The country itself was enemy

1

enough, and the Apaches thought it was theirs. A lone white man had to be very sure of what he was doing if he wanted to come back with his hair on the top of his head where nature had put it.

Winters Dave worked for a grub stake at four dollars a day, and these last months he had dreamed of May when he could draw his pay and cut southward for the San Pedro hills.

So he laughed and waved off the good-humored jibes of the crew and walked another half mile to the cabin he had found abandoned and had preempted at the north edge of the straggling town.

He pushed open the sagging door and went in. It was no warmer inside. His morning fire in the sheet-iron stove had long since gotten lonesome and died. The cabin was also dark. The sun was gone and the single small window let in very little light. He picked the lamp out of its wall bracket, set it on the table, lifted the smoked chimney and struck a match.

There was a scrabbling as a pack rat hurried to its hiding place somewhere in the rafters. Dave swore at it because last night it had made off with one of his socks and he had not yet found it.

He turned to build his fire then, and saw the man in his bunk. For an instant alarm bells rang and he stood very still, then anger came and he started across the narrow room with his hand stretched to jerk the blanket off the

2

brazen intruder.

But as he reached the bunk his hand dropped. The man was very old, with dark skin drawn tight over sunken cheeks and toothless jaws, with thin hair long and straight and white. A Mexican from the looks of him, and Harden was not too fond of Mexicans. He was asleep, his breathing so shallow that the blanket barely rose and fell.

Dave started again for the stove and his foot kicked the box he used as a chair. He caught his balance and looked toward the bunk. The old man's eyes were open, dark and overbright with undisguised fear. They made Dave feel guilty. The man was so small, so shrunken. The little mound he made under the cover was not five feet long, and if he weighed ninety pounds he must have swallowed a sledgehammer. He laid the blanket back and sat up with a slow cringing and spoke in a hoarse whisper that quavered.

'I am sorry, Señor. I did not mean to be here when you came. But I was so tired . . . so cold.'

His shoulders hunched, shuddered with chill. Dave smiled to knock down the fear, went to the stove and built a quick, hot fire. When the wood was crackling, the flames jumping and the fire box beginning to throw out heat, he looked back at the bunk. The visitor sat on the edge with his feet hanging and the blanket hugged around him. Beneath

3

the coppery tone his face had a gray pallor.

Dave kept a bottle of whiskey hidden for emergencies. This looked like an emergency and he got it out, poured a drink for his visitor and, as a kind of afterthought, poured one for himself. He watched the man sip it, making it last, making the most of its warmth.

'Hungry?'

The eyes answered him. He took a knife and went outside. One of the boys had got a fat buck the day before and had given Dave a haunch. He had hung it in one of the aspens, out on a limb where a prowling animal could not get at it. He cut a steak.

He put the meat in the deep iron frying pot, scooped beans in with it to reheat and made camp biscuits. All through these preparations he felt the old eyes follow him, but after his first speech the ancient made no sound.

He ate sparingly, slowly, like a man starved but whose stomach was too shrunk to tolerate much food at one time. When he had finished, there was a trace of color in his face. He said very simply, 'Señor, you are good.'

Dave Harden was embarrassed, remembering his first impulse to boot the stranger out into the snow, and to cover it he asked, 'You come far?'

A withered talon the color of old ivory gestured toward the south. 'A long way. Yes.'

'Where are you going?'

The man was silent for a spell, his eyes

4

going around the room as if looking for a destination and he sagged lower.

'I had a cousin. I came to find him here. At the mine office they told me he died last year. Then I had no place to go, no money.'

Harden was jolted by the thought that he could well be saddled with this oldster and said quickly, 'Where are your other relatives?'

The white head moved from side to side. 'There is no one left.'

Silence filled the room. Even the pack rat was quiet. The only sounds were the creak of the cabin walls and the gusting of the evening wind trying to push them over.

Then Harden said, 'What do you intend to do?'

The head shook. The hands spread, palms up.

Impatience filled Dave Harden. He wondered if the old coot was trying to play him for a sucker. But he had been hungry himself, and the idea of turning the shriveled Mexican out into the cold night did not fit with his nature.

'Well,' he said, 'you can stay here for a few weeks with me. When I leave you can have the cabin, but I don't know what you'll eat then.'

'I thank you.'

Dave got up to clean the dishes and the old man said in a musing voice, 'You are quitting the mine soon? Why?'

'Soon as the weather breaks. I'm a

prospector.' Dave was busy, not looking at him. 'I was raised in Gold Hill on the Rogue in southern Oregon. My father was a forty-niner. His luck was thin in California and he kept moving north, landed on the Rogue. I grew up hunting gold. Still doing it.' Even talking about it brought a lift to his voice.

The musing tone pried further. 'You have found much?'

'A little. Never a big strike yet. But this season I'll make it.'

There was a soft, private, satisfied sound from the old man and Harden looked around. He found him fumbling inside his limp shirt and thought he was probing for a flea, but then the claw hands dug out a buckskin pouch on a leather thong, worked the thong over his head and opened the purse mouth in his lap. Delicately the fingers searched, withdrew a parchment folded many times and held it toward Harden. The old man made a shrug to deprecate the act of giving and his eyes begged that the gift would be accepted.

'I will never use it,' he said. 'I am too old. But you . . . young, strong . . . I give you the map to Tayopa.'

Dave Harden stared, feeling a little giddy for the instant. Anyone who had spent any time in the villages along the border had heard the fables of the legendary Tayopa. Then his common sense took hold. Men had been hunting that lost mine for a couple of centuries

6

and no one had ever yet located it. It was a myth, another barroom fairy tale. He backed away a step from the extended hand.

'You'd better sell it for eating money, Pop. There's lots of greenhorns itching to buy maps like that.'

The Mexican did not take offense but smiled his understanding of Harden's doubt.

'I know, Señor. The many stories that tantalize, and the discouraging evidence that in Mexico City there are no records to say such a place ever existed . . . but it did . . .'

Harden shook his head, smiling to take the bite out of his disbelief.

'It's a pretty dream all right and I appreciate your offer, but I've had some experience looking into those Mexican files. You know, the Spanish king took a cut of one-fifth of all minerals mined in Mexico, and the records of every mine, some of them still operating today, run back without a break to the time of Cortés. And there isn't a single mention of a Tayopa.'

'Granted.' A touch of humor put some life in the faded eyes. 'The official records are indeed silent. But Tayopa was worked by the Jesuits. You know, perhaps, that the Society of Jesus was a very secretive order?'

Harden felt a laugh and let it come. 'You're saying that the good padres held out on the King of Spain?'

'Sí, Señor. I know that at Tayopa mines

7

were worked for over fifteen years. And in all that time not one ounce of silver was shipped out from them. It was not unusual for the Church to circumvent the King, no?

'Maybe I tell you what you already know, but in 1593 the King decreed that priests could no longer continue to own mines. That decree was ignored, and issued again in 1621 and ignored, and not until 1703 was it made effective.'

The night was full of surprises for Dave. This apparent vagabond knew his history. It flustered Harden and, to get himself adjusted to the idea, he went for a glass, poured a little whiskey into it and filled it with hot water from the pan on the stove, then put the toddy into the old hands.

The man drank gratefully and made a sucking noise with his thin lips. The color in his face was better, but a long way from good.

Harden sat down on the foot of the bunk. The old man was well spoken, obviously educated. In spite of himself Dave felt excitement taking hold of him. There was something about lost mines and buried treasures that got into a man's blood. He found himself listening with closer attention.

'So,' said the old man, 'the Jesuits closed their mines to wait until the King's order was rescinded. They hid the silver that had accumulated and filled the entrances of their shafts and tunnels to hide them. They meant to return, but that never happened. The Apaches came raiding. They murdered the Indian slaves who had worked the mines. They pulled down the buildings. They destroyed Tayopa and took it out of the living world and lost it.'

'Why?'

'Who knows why the Apache does anything he does?'

'And how do you know all this?'

The old head was nodding in the manner of the storyteller. 'I have spent my life trying to unravel the mystery of Tayopa. My interest began when I was very young, when I became caretaker of an ancient church, one of the first the Spaniards built in the Sierra Madre. The padres were good to me. They taught me to read and write, they educated me. I learned much more than anyone else of my family.

'There was silver in my church, ornaments, a wrought-silver railing, more silver in the vaults. Yet our area was poor. I began to wonder where it came from. Then in the sacristy I found records, very old records, of births and baptisms and marriages and deaths, very complete and precise. Then I discovered the itemized tallies of all the gold and silver that had been taken from the mines of Tayopa. The name was there to read. And I found the map.' He caught Dave's hand and closed it around the parchment.

'What you hold there is a true copy of the

9

map I found. I have seen many others in my wandering, but this one I believe is the only true picture of the way to Tayopa.'

Harden unfolded the map as if it might bite him and saw that it was elaborately drawn. Not only were the heights of mountains indicated but also their longitude and latitude.

His mouth was dry enough so that he had to moisten it before he could ask the questions that were crowding him.

'Why did you copy it if the padres were so good to you?'

The sunken face wrinkled into a grimace. 'Those priests went away. A foreigner came in their place, an Italian who made life miserable for all of us. So I copied the map and left and went to Mexico City. In the records there I found nothing about Tayopa. I went looking, many other places. In Nacori Chico I found more records, including some drawn by the curia in Tayopa . . . also at Bacadeguachi.

'So, Señor, there was a Tayopa. And it had to be a very important place. There were not three other curas in the whole region.'

It all had the ring of truth about it and Harden had no doubt that the old man believed what he was saying. But Dave had hunted for other lost mines and he knew that man's memory was not always trustworthy. There was another cause for suspicion, and he asked the question casually, as if it were not important.

10

'With the map . . . with being so sure about it, why didn't you go to Tayopa yourself?'

The old man worked his hands in a wringing of frustration.

'The Indians, Señor. The Yaquis have never yet been conquered and the Apaches even now raid at their whim. Mexico was in tumult and the soldiers spent their time killing each other. None of them would move against the Indians. I waited for peace and order to come. I waited too long. Now I am too old. I will never see Tayopa.'

Harden's ears were ringing as if his head would burst. 'Maybe you will,' he said. 'Maybe you and I might just travel down there and see what we can find . . . Take the bunk. Get some sleep. We'll talk about it in the morning.'

They did not talk about it in the morning. In the morning the old man was dead.


CHAPTER TWO

There are two mountain ranges in Mexico that are called the Sierra Madres. One, in the southeast, parallels the Gulf of Mexico and enjoys a tropical climate, is well watered and offers an easy place to live.

The Sierra Madre del Norte is a very different matter. It rises in northern Chihuahua and Sonora out of high, bleak desert on either side and runs southward generally following the Gulf of California, slicing northern Mexico into east and west parts that have almost no communication with each other.

Almost impossible to cross, it is a spine of formidable mile-high mountains, mile-deep canyons, jumbled badlands and surprising lush and fertile valleys, beginning some two hundred kilometers west of Chihuahua City and towering up in a series of sharp, cruel ridges. It is a land apart, an entity in itself. And it is the home of three separate Indian nations.

On the high, timbered mesas of the east slope are the sorry remnants of the Tarahumares. Once a numerous people, these were among the first to be reduced by the early Spaniards and enslaved to work in the rich mines and the luxuriant haciendas in the canyon valleys.

To the west of them are the tribeless Opathas. Both peoples are decimated, their blood mixed, Mexicanized so thoroughly that very few pure *indios* remain. Their histories are lost and in some places even their languages are forgotten in the mists of time.

Down the west slope is Yaqui country. Cousins of the Apaches, the Yaquis are a fierce, proud, independent people whom neither the Spaniard nor later the Mexican government ever conquered. They are raised from babyhood to hate and mistrust anyone with European blood and travel through their territory is for fools.

The Sierra Madre del Norte is a forgotten world, bypassed by history for over two hundred years.

And yet this silent, brooding, forbidding land was, prior to 1600, the richest, most highly civilized and productive area of all Mexico. Its mines gave up more gold and silver than any other region of North America. Its haciendas were cornucopias of grain and fruit and cattle. Every Pueblo boasted a church, some small, some thriving, depending on the local productivity.

What happened? What made a ghost world of the Sierra Madre, a wilderness of empty badlands, its mined pueblos sinking into the rich earth, its mines lost to memory? What left its natives impoverished, crouching in hidden caves far from traveled trails, eking out an existence with no tools, machinery or guns, answering the questions of outsiders with blank, empty faces?

First, in the early 1600s, the brutally ground-down slaves revolted. They wiped out their masters at the mines, massacred the big landholders and their families and sent the diminished Spanish forces reeling south for safety.

The revolt was not a total success. Many of the Jesuit Order survived and prevailed. The most militant of the Catholic orders, these priests had pioneered the region, spread through the mountains, built pueblos, converted the natives and made slaves of them, operated mines, founded churches, administered their domain for the enrichment of their Order with little attention to the laws of the Spanish empire. Their hold on the proselytized Indians was stronger than any other force in Spanish Mexico and they had long been a thorn in the side of the civil and military authorities. They resisted the revolt and resisted the several Spanish attempts to wrest their mines from them for another hundred years.

Then the ban that barred any church or churchman from owning mines was successfully enforced. The priests were driven out. They went methodically, hid the precious metals already mined and not exported, concealed the mines themselves, took their maps and directions for relocating the properties to be ready for such time as the ban might be lifted, and departed.

They left behind their Indian neophytes, only partly civilized and having lost their tribal unity and ancient self-sufficiency. The abandoned, hapless people then fell easy prey to a new enemy—the Apaches.

For a thousand years these pirates of the desert had raided southward from their Arizona strongholds, sweeping through the pueblos, stealing horses, women, children for slaves, murdering the men.

As long as the mines were active and the haciendas strong these raids had met with fierce resistance, but with the Jesuits gone and the country in chaos the forays from the north raced unchecked, destroying everything in their paths, wiping out whole towns, razing the buildings, leaving behind a wasteland and a decimated, demoralized, defenseless population that crept back into the hills like animals for what little security they could find.

The Mexican authorities reacted by offering a bounty of one hundred dollars for every Apache scalp or head brought to the government palace in Chihuahua City and into that tortured land rode a new group of ruthless and violent men—the scalp hunters.

Their names are terror. James Kirker. Chief Spiebuck. Captain Hobbs and his seventy Delaware braves. Casimero Streeter, called the White Apache, who gave his name to the language, for in northern Mexico Streeter became the common term for bandit.

They fringed the window frames of the palace with festoons of hair. They picketed the plaza with tall spikes, raw heads impaled on their tops. And they were careless of what they sold. Native Indian hair looked the same as Apache hair.

Whatever virtue the program had, the American Civil War interrupted it, pulled most of the men off the troubled border and left the

Apaches free to raid and burn and kill with little interference.

So in the early seventies the Sierra Madre del Norte lay prostrate, bleeding, the people powerless to protect themselves, powerless to do more than hide from any enemy. And even the glittering vision of hidden treasures, of ancient mines tempted few to venture in.

\*　　\*　　\*

Dave Harden knew the history. He knew that having a map was not the same thing as having a mine. Dave had ridden the high country of Oregon. He had prospected through Colorado and Nevada, and hunted the Dragoons and the San Pedro hills of southern Arizona. And he had never seen anything as barren, as bleak, as empty, as haunted as the Sierra Madre.

Having a map was one thing, following it was another. On the morning when he had found the old Mexican dead he had put aside any thought of hunting for the lost mines of Tayopa. He had finished out his contract at the McCracken, bought his supplies, loaded his pack mule and headed for the San Pedro. He rode past Martinez, Hassayampa, on to Wickenburg. And in a saloon in Wickenburg he had listened as a drunk retold to the room full of men the glowing legend of Tayopa.

Small things change a man's mind. Later, in the narrow hotel room, Dave Harden pulled

16

out the old parchment. There was writing on it, ancient writing in a copperplate, slanting script. Dave had picked up a smattering of *cholo* along the border, but this was Spanish that he could not translate.

The next day he started for El Paso, for the easiest way into the Sierra Madre was said to be through Chihuahua City.

He was three weeks on the road and he spent another week in the city, locating a clerk in the office of land deeds who could translate the writing on his map. Dave was a careful man. He did not go into anything without considering it from all angles, without preparation.

He saw the old scalps and the rotting heads fencing the plaza. He listened to the talk in the cantinas about the dangers of the Sierra Madre. He heard that the Apaches had been bad that spring. Then he went back to confer with the clerk and pay him fifty pesos for his information.

The man had been there a long time, and was well learned. He admitted that he had seen other maps purporting to show the road to Tayopa and said that this one looked more authentic than most. He would not try to go there for all of the thirty million pesos of silver the parchment said was buried under the church.

The map was dated at Tayopa in 1703 and the directions were specific enough, including the longitude and latitude of what mountains would be passed and should serve as guide. The opening instruction was to stand on the Cerro de la Campana at sunset, directly facing the setting sun. Tayopa would be eight-days' travel toward that sunset.

Dave asked if the clerk knew of a Cerro de la Campana and the man went to search the records. He came back to report that the only Cerro de la Campana in Chihuahua he could find was a hill whose name had been changed in recent times to the Cerro de Minaca, that it was a little south of Guerrero, which was some two hundred kilometers west of Chihuahua.

Dave Harden paid him, thanked him and left. He bought fresh supplies, including a case of dynamite that he broke open and loaded on his mule. Then he rode to Minaca.

He found the *cerro* without difficulty, a hill shaped like a loaf of bread, rising abruptly from the level plain. He climbed it to the top. His methodical mind made him follow the instructions to the letter. That was the way a good prospector worked, studying each step as he went.

The map had been dated March seventeenth. Did that mean Tayopa would lie in the path of the setting sun only on that date? For in that latitude the sun shifted far north during the summer, and it was now nearly the last of May.

One item seemed more important than the

position of the sun. The old Sonora trail started at Minaca and wound west into the Sierra Madre. It was an ancient trail and had had many names. The early Spaniards had called it El Camino Real, the Royal Highway. It was neither a highway nor had royalty ever set foot on it.

It was a slender thread cut deep in soil and rock by the sharp hoofs of burro trains that for a hundred years had carried supplies into the mines and brought out enormous loads of heavy gold and silver.

Harden took the old road early in the morning. The eight days specified on the map should mean about two hundred miles. He was in no hurry. He had heard no reports of Apaches in Minaca, although this was not to be relied on. The raiders seldom showed themselves in the foothill towns.

Dave Harden respected Apaches but he did not fear them. If a man was well armed, if he were careful . . . He had prospected in their northern country for several years without serious trouble.

The Royal Highway, never wide, narrowed as he climbed the first ridges of the Sierra. For miles on end it rose through deep gorges and along the edge of precipices without room to turn a horse except at points where dim side tracks that might be either animal or human trails cut away and disappeared among tumbled, flinty ridges.

19

For five days he climbed steadily and did not see a human being, heard nothing but a mournful wind that moaned among the rocks. He had been told that there were people in the mountains but that he was unlikely to see them. They lived far back from the road, would spot a stranger before he could discover them and fade off into the rocky wastes. They were, he understood, not warlike, wanted no contact with any traveler. They were not a danger. Danger would only come from small bands of raiding Apaches.

Still he rode watchfully, across timbered mesas, through forests of giant pines. For half a day he twisted down as the trail descended into the canyon of the Mayo, where wild cotton trees were thick, their trunks and branches studded with sharp spines that seemed to reach out to catch at his clothes.

He watered his horse and pack mule at the crystal stream, then climbed again through a grove of shining, evergreen madroños burdened with hundreds of silkworm cocoons. And at the crest he came to a fork in the trail.

He sat studying the roads. Both looked evenly traveled. Both were chiseled deep in living rock by thousands of hoofs. It was impossible to tell which scars were fresh, which were two hundred years old.

The mood of the land began to oppress him. Like all prospectors he was a natural loner, but even in the Arizona hills there was the sense that other people might be near. Here was a spookiness, a vast, dead emptiness that he had never felt before.

He picketed his animals in a small bowl behind the fork, ate his meal in silent solitude, then climbed a rock face to find a sleeping place in a nest of boulders. Only a fool camped near his animals in Apache country. An Indian could locate picketed horses almost by instinct, but a man in a fireless camp, hidden at a distance, might sleep in peace if he knew that he would wake as soon as an Indian found his animals.

In the morning he chose the fork that curved a little north and spent a fruitless day following it to a ruined pueblo. Alone in the grass-grown street he looked at the church, roofless, its empty bell tower still intact. He looked where 'dobe buildings had gradually melted into shapeless forms, saw huge trees growing up in the ruins, trees that by their size must be over a hundred years old.

People had been here and were not here now. The place brought the emptiness into sharp focus. His oppression crowded on him, settled into a hunger to talk to someone, anyone.

He found people to talk to the next day. Two short, flat-faced men had come down from their village somewhere back in the mountains to meet the mail carrier. Harden had been told about these monthly mails that traveled the road between Chihuahua and distant Hermosillo. The mail was carried by a sandaled mozo with a little mule. Even the Indians were said not to attack the mail, knowing that if the carrier did not arrive at his destination an armed force would be sent out to search for him.

The three did not vanish. They watched Harden come, human beings in white shirts, loose cotton trousers and woven sandals. The round Indian faces showed neither pleasure nor fear at his arrival. They had nothing. They would not be robbed. There would be no point in this gringo harming them.

They sat in the shade of a great pile of loose rocks, watching as he got down and went to squat at their side. They even spoke, explaining in slow Spanish that they had come down expecting a letter from a brother in Hermosillo who was now a priest. They told him the rock pile represented a shrine. Whose shrine it was they did not know. That knowledge had been lost before their grandfather's time. What lingered was the custom that any traveler passing here should add a stone to the pile. Judging by the size of the heap the custom went back to the beginning of time.

The ageless qualities of these hills came home again to Harden. Time meant nothing to these people. They lived from sunrise until sunset. They did not look for the lost riches that had been hidden in the earth. They made no effort to revitalize the ruined ranches in the rich canyons. They ate when they could find something to eat. When they could not, they went hungry.

He offered his tobacco. It was accepted gravely and the four of them smoked in silence, like four friends who have known each other so long they needed no words to communicate. They did not ask what he was doing in the Sierra. They saw his pick and shovel on the burro. It told them all they wanted to know.

'Did you ever hear of Tayopa?' He asked it of them all but looked at the elder brother.

The empty faces emptied further.

In Chihuahua the clerk had warned him. 'The people won't talk about the old mines. Many of them know where some old shaft is, but a mass memory is graven into them. Their ancestors showed the Spaniards and the priests where there was gold and silver and the ancestors were enslaved. Gold and silver mean slavery to them. Mines mean slavery. They do not want the mines reopened. Sometimes one of them will bring in a handful, buy a few things, go to the cantina and treat until the bartender says he has used his metal up, then he'll disappear into the hills again. You'll get no help from them.'

'I have heard the name.' The older brother stood up without haste. 'We do not know

23

where it is, Señor, if it exists. No one knows. Thank you for the tobacco.'

The other Indian rose and followed the first around the shrine. *Vaya con Dios.'*

They were gone. Harden watched until he could see no more movement among the tumbled boulders. When he turned back the mail mozo was on his mule, his feet dangling close to the ground, slowly jogging east. Within five minutes Harden was alone again in the sullen mountain silence.


## CHAPTER THREE

He had crossed the high crest and turned down the western slope of the range, looking out to a horizon where the blue of sky and the blue of mountains melded and he could not tell where the line of demarkation was. Between there and where he sat stretched a frozen raging sea of lesser crests like hurricane-thrown waves, a much longer slope than the sharp eastern rise.

Three days after he had met the Indians he picketed his animals in a small draw and climbed up to sleep on the hogback above it. The trail bent around the nose of the hogback and from the top he looked across a shallow, barren canyon and could see the trail climb the far side, a mile away.

He waked early and as he rolled out of his blanket his eye caught movement, as of a fly crawling on a distant wall. At first he could not locate it when he looked directly; it was only hinted at in his peripheral vision. He stayed where he was.

Later he spotted it, a black speck on the trail, moving toward him, coming from the west. The speck grew slowly and became a horse and rider advancing steadily but in no hurry. Later still he could tell by the way the rider sat, straight-backed in the saddle, that it was neither an Indian nor a Mexican.

He had no glasses. He could not guess the man's identity or errand. It might be an American like himself also looking for a lost mine, perhaps Tayopa itself. It could be a renegade or a criminal dodging the law above the border, for although the Streeter gang had long since been broken up there were still many Americans south of the line who dared not go home.

Harden was not worried. It would be a chance to talk to someone human, and he felt confident that he could handle any situation that might rise.

The hogback was two hundred feet above his animals with rocks and brush enough to screen him. He kept down, watched the traveler disappear into a dip of the trail then lift out of it considerably closer. Now he could see the head below the hat. The man was

25

black.

He sat tall in the saddle, a powerfully built man who rode with the stiff back of a cavalryman, and now as he neared the rock shoulder of the draw that hid Harden's horse Dave saw that he wore a black cavalry hat, the blue jacket and lighter blue kersey trousers.

The rider, still unaware of Harden, came around the bend, saw the picketed animals, and stopped. He sat still in his saddle, only his head slowly turning, searching among the rocks on both sides of the draw.

Harden stood up. The man's eyes lifted and found him. After a moment the tensed shoulders relaxed a little as if he recognized another American when he had feared something else.

'Well, Captain.' The relief in the voice could not be mistaken.

Harden lifted a hand in casual greeting and carefully worked down to the bottom of the draw. The big man had swung out of his saddle but stood close to his horse as if not certain of his welcome.

Harden had studied him closely as be came down, had seen the cartridge belt around the strong waist, with the regulation flap holster. He was willing to bet that the holster held an army Peacemaker Colt .45 rather than the civilian Frontier version, the .44. And the barrel that hung through the open bottom of the holster was a good seven and a half inches long, not the five-and-a-half-inch artillery model.

The brim of the black campaign hat was pinned up in front by a crossed saber emblem with a small figure ten between the hilts.

The jacket was open, the high collar unhooked, showing the gray flannel shirt beneath. And on the jacket sleeve were unfaded stripes where hash marks had been torn away. The trousers were faded, stained with dirt and much riding. The clothes, Harden thought, told the story of the man.

'Deserter?'

The dark eyes flicked. The firm but mobile mouth tightened and the coffee-colored face became a mask.

'You might say that, Captain.'

Harden was suddenly irritated. Like most men on the fringes of the frontier he had little love for soldiers. He knew they were necessary, that without the string of forts no one would be safe from Indian attack, but he had a poor opinion of a man who would take orders for thirteen dollars a month.

'Don't call me that. I'm not in the army.'

'No, sir.' The mellow voice was neutral.

'Don't call me *sir* either. The name is Harden. Dave Harden.'

'Pleased to make your acquaintance, Mr. Harden.'

Dave could not be certain whether or not the black man was mocking him. He put it

27

aside as unimportant. There were amenities of the trail to observe.

'You eaten today?'

'No, sir. I rode through the night. I was just looking for a place to camp.'

'And I'm ready for breakfast. You get some wood while I stir up the biscuits.'

The black man dipped his head, tugged on the reins and led his horse to the trickle of a stream that leaked from a wet seep in the rocks. He pulled off the saddle. Then he peeled out of his jacket and gathered dry wood.

Harden had shot a small *jabalina* the day before, had cooked the chops for his supper and smoked one of the hams over a brush fire. He sliced the pork now into the skillet, put biscuits in the deep iron pan to bake and made coffee.

He had only one cup, one plate. The Negro brought his own from the roll behind his saddle. Dave was amused that they were government issue. The ex-sergeant appeared to have equipped himself from the quartermaster's stores.

He dished up smoking meat, soaked biscuits in the hot grease and poured coffee. 'All right, Sergeant, pitch in.'

The Negro tasted the meat and showed his pleasure. 'First ham I've seen in a long time. Where'd you get it?'

'Shot it yesterday.'

The dark eyes widened in surprise. 'You mean it? There's wild pigs down here?'

Harden, enjoying the sound of human voices, used the question as an excuse to talk on.

'Sure. They're a big delicacy with the natives. They haven't got guns, so they figured out their own way of getting them. Drive them into a cave then block up the entrance and build a fire, fill the cave with smoke and smother the pig.'

'Nothing wrong with that. Man, am I going to watch for one of these.'

'Don't go after it on foot. I heard about one that killed a dog and when the man went after it with a machete he was gored. He died of it.'

'Bad. That's bad. I'll remember that, Mr. Harden.'

He went back to eating, savoring the sweet meat. There was a quiet confidence about him that sat well with Harden. Dave tried to guess what he was doing in this wild land. That he had crossed the Yaqui country by traveling at night told that he knew something about those Indians and their dislike of moving in the darkness. And it was not odd that an army deserter should head below the border.

But why had he not stayed in Hermosillo or gone on to Guaymas? Why turn aside into the wilderness of the Sierra? Of course the answer might be in his earlier thought that the man could be looking for treasure.

The notes on Harden's map claimed that there was thirty-million-pesos' worth of gold and silver buried under the floor of the Tayopa church. Dave did not trust the figure but if the mine had been in bonanza for fifteen yeas and none of the bullion had been shipped there ought to be enough for two men to share.

But he wanted to know more about this man before he suggested that they join forces.

'What's your name, Sergeant?'

The big man's head came up and there was a short hesitation. 'You figuring maybe you can send me back?'

Harden shook his head, laughing. 'I don't knew what you're doing in this tag end of the world, but one thing I'm not doing is rounding up anybody for the army. You can believe that.'

The ex-sergeant relaxed again. 'They call me Purdy. Luke Purdy.'

'That your name?'

The black man grinned. 'It's as good as any, Mr. Harden. As good as any. One thing a free man can do is choose what name he likes. Ain't that so?'

'Why, I guess so.' A quarter of the people Harden had met on the frontier had changed their names for reasons of their own. 'I never considered it much. Never had any reason not to use the name my daddy gave me.'

He rose and went to get fresh tobacco from his pack. When he lifted the tarpaulin it uncovered the pick, the shovel, the dynamite sticks packed in the burlap sacks. He brought the tobacco back and offered it. The Negro accepted it with an appreciative grunt.

'You going mining down here, Mr. Harden?'

His eyes, his attention were on rolling the cigarette, licking it, picking a live coal from the fire with a calloused thumb and forefinger, dragging smoke in deep. Harden guessed that he was starved for the taste of tobacco, and judging from the size of the bedroll behind the high cavalry saddle the man was short of provisions of any kind.

He did not answer the question and Purdy did not pursue it. He finished the cigarette, regretfully tossed the stub into the fire as it singed his lips, stood up and stretched his powerful arms wide.

'Guess I'll hide the horse and catch some sleep. I've been moving nights. Heard the Yaquis were bad but they don't like to be around much after dark, that they think dead men's spirits ride the trails then. This country's spooky enough to believe it, too.'

'Emptiest-feeling place I ever saw.'

Purdy blew out a sharp breath. 'You can say that again, and still I feel like eyes keep watching me while I ride down this lonesome old trail. Like haunts.'

Harden smiled, recognizing his own reaction to these mountains.

'They aren't haunts. They're real enough,

31

and they are watching, but only so they can stay out of your way. A clerk in Chihuahua told me there are still a lot of people up here, though nothing like there were a couple of hundred years ago. The place was crawling with them then, a lot of mines were running. Mule trains thirty burros long kept this trail hot. The priests who ran the show kept riding back and forth on big black oxen.'

'Think of that.' Purdy squatted again, putting off his sleep.

Harden propped his shoulders against a boulder, the pictures building in his mind, not wanting to let go of this human contact.

'There was lots going on then. Besides the mines there were towns, and ranches, big spreads in all the canyons, raising cattle, growing orchards of oranges and quinces, bananas, everything . . .'

Purdy whistled softly. 'That just don't seem possible. Not from the way it looks now. I haven't seen a soul. Tell me, Mr. Harden, did you meet many people coming across?'

'No. And will you stop calling me Mr. Harden. Every time you say it I look around to see if my old man is standing behind me. When we were kids he used to make us all call him *mister.* Said it was more respectful. I got my bellyful of it.'

The black man's laugh was full-bodied, delighted, as if for the first time since he had ridden in he was genuinely amused. Then he sobered.

'You didn't meet anybody?'

'Only a couple of peons down to meet the mail mozo. Why? You expecting to meet somebody down here?'

'Who, me?' Purdy rolled his eyes extravagantly. 'What would a man like me be doing, expecting to meet somebody around here?'

He laughed, trying to sound convincing. Dave Harden decided that whatever else Luke Purdy was, he was not a good liar.

## CHAPTER FOUR

Purdy put his horse in the draw and climbed to the hogback where Harden had slept. Dave Harden packed his mule and headed west, saying nothing about a partnership.

He rode half of the forenoon. The taste of companionship in this eerie land followed him and increased his sense that he was moving through a void. His horse slowed and then stopped, finding no command from its preoccupied rider.

Harden came to with a start, sat a moment longer, then abruptly put the animal about and went back.

The big black man heard him come, sat up and called down. 'You forget something,

Dave?'

Harden sat his horse, sent his words up to the rocks.

'Maybe yes, maybe no. I came back to ask if you want to throw in with me.'

Purdy stood up slowly, put his fists on his hips and looked down, silent for a long moment before he said, 'You mean go mining?'

'I mean look for gold and silver that's already mined. Thirty-million-pesos' worth of it.'

Purdy continued standing, then, deliberately he came down to the trail.

'Thirty million. How much is that in American money today?'

Harden stepped out of his saddle, saying over his shoulder, 'I don't know what a peso was worth when the treasure was hidden but I'd say it was enough. More than two men could spend in a lifetime.'

'I'm listening. Tell me about it.'

Harden talked through the afternoon, about the history of the land, the priests, the Indian slaves, the Apaches. He did not mention the map. That he held out as a precaution against the chance that a man whom he knew so little about might be the kind who would want to take the whole find for himself.

'It's up to you,' he said finally. 'This is a lonesome damned country and I'd just as soon have a man beside me who knows how to ride, can handle a gun and who isn't afraid of hard work. Do you want to come?'

The Negro sat silent, studying the ground for a long time. Then hesitantly, as if he thought it might be refused, he thrust out his hand.

Harden took it. His fingers were strong. Luke Purdy's were stronger. Harden's hand tingled for minutes after the grip was broken. He flexed the fingers, disguising the exercise in unloading his mule. Together they built up the fire and made an evening meal.

Afterward, sitting across the dying flames from each other, Harden looked at the man over the rim of his coffee cup.

'I told you what I'm doing. I invited you in. Maybe I'd feel better about it if I thought you trusted me.'

Purdy met his look without expression. 'Meaning?'

'All I know about you is that you deserted from the army. That's not much of a recommendation for a partner in a treasure hunt. You want to tell me why?'

'Why I deserted or what I'm doing down here?'

'Both, if they aren't the same thing.'

Purdy took his time. Harden had about decided that he had made a mistake, that the man would not answer. He waited while Purdy rolled a cigarette; smoked it to the last half inch and snapped it at the fire.

'What would you say if I told you I was out to kill a man? A white man? Would you try to stop me?'

'Depends on how good a reason you got.'

'I've got a reason. The best. Only maybe a white man wouldn't think so.'

'I don't know what the color of a man's skin has to do with how he thinks.'

Now there was urgency in the voice. 'It does. Dave. It does. No one who's not black knows what it means . . . Anyhow, you know what slave catchers are . . . were?'

'I guess so. I'm from Oregon. We didn't have slaves up there or slave catchers either.'

'Well, before the War there were bastards in the East who made a living running down escaped slaves and taking them back for the rewards. They didn't stop with that. When they could they kidnapped black people who had their free papers, hauled them south and sold them back into slavery.'

Harden frowned into the fire. 'I don't see how they could do that.'

'Oh, they did it all right. Worse than your scalp hunters taking Mexican Indians' hair and passing it off for Apache.

'So. My ma and pa got their papers and me and my sister were born free. We all went north and my pa got a job in a shipyard. There was a runaway nigger working there, and two slave catchers came up after him. They spotted my pa. They followed him home. They broke

36

in in the middle of the night. Kidnapped my pa and ma and sister. She was fourteen.'

He was silent, his eyes catching the red of the fire, reflecting it.

'They took their papers and burned them. Loaded my folks into a wagon and headed south. One of them raped my sister. Maybe both of them. She don't remember too much about that night. Then my pa made a break and they shot him. They took my mother and sister on and sold them in Mississippi.'

Harden swore softly to himself.

Purdy was talking again, the flat voice no longer steady. 'I was in Canada. I didn't know a thing about it. That was the year before the War. After the War I got a letter from my sister. She was still in Mississippi, said ma had died. I sent her money to come and join me.

'She told me about the men, their names, where they came from. I went down there and learned they'd headed west for Arizona Territory. So I joined the Tenth Cavalry, figured it would give me a reason to be in the country while I hunted for them.'

'You didn't find them?'

'I found one. Tending bar in Tucson. I won't tell you how I killed him, but he told me his old partner was working for some ranch back in the Sierra Madres. He didn't know where the ranch was, but I'll find him if he's in here.'

Harden, looking at the face across the fire, was certain that he would.

37

Purdy reached to pour more coffee. 'That's it. You want to change your mind?'

Harden moved his head from side to side and Purdy's mouth loosened, lifted.

'Which way do we go?'

Harden threw more wood on the fire for better light and now he brought out his map, hunched around to Purdy's side and spread it to the ground. With his blunt finger he traced the faded lines.

'I figure we're about here. The way the map reads, Tayopa was somewhere along the headwaters of the Yaqui River, north of this trail. So I'd say the thing to do is push west to the Yaqui then hunt for a way north, through the mountains. Tayopa must have been tied to this road by a mule trail.

'It won't be easy. If it were it would have been found long ago.'

'All right. It sounds as good a way as any for me to start looking. I don't care about the money. I want to find Seth Slade, though he's probably not using that name now.'

Harden folded the map, put it back in the pouch. 'You know what he looks like?'

'No, I don't. I do know one thing about him. He's lost two toes off his left foot.'

They headed west at first light. The trail pinched in, too narrow to ride abreast. Harden took the lead through the morning, Purdy through the afternoon. That night they camped against the Papigochic River in some of the wildest land Harden had seen yet. Two more days took them to the crossing of the Yaqui, and there they found a little-used trace winding north. It took them up at a steep climb through gullies between great buttresses of stone, a path so narrow that in places the pack on the mule scraped both sides of the walls.

Late afternoon brought them to a fork, one arm of which angled back toward the east. The other kept a northerly course, more or less following the line of the river that was now far below.

Harden chose that and they continued climbing for two miles without breaking out of the close, confining walls. Then a steep side draw opened off to their left, a dry stream bed with a small leveled space washed out at its mouth.

'Hold up.' Purdy halted his horse, his voice running back softly to Harden, his face tipped up at the draw.

After a minute Harden saw it, a little doe halfway up the slope, her head turned toward them, ears cocked forward.

Purdy loosened his carbine, raised it slowly. The shot was long for the short-barreled gun and its heavy-grained bullet.

The report bounced around among the rock walls like a volley. The deer stood for a full moment, not moving. Harden thought Purdy had missed, then the animal pitched, fell halfway down the steep incline and lay wedged behind a big boulder.

Purdy shoved the gun back into the scabbard, swung down and scrambled up the rock face, having to use his hands more than his feet. Harden watched the perfect coordination that made the climb look easy.

Purdy hung with one hand against the rocks, worked the deer free with the other and dropped it down. He followed, then used his knife to cut the throat, and hung the deer from a branch of a wind-warped pine tree. He let it bleed and turned to where Harden had dismounted.

'Camp here?'

'Could be the only place wide enough we'd find before dark.'

Dave unsaddled the horses and pulled off the mule's pack while Purdy skinned the doe. He cut thick steaks from one hindquarter, carved out the liver and sliced it into a pan. Then, with the fire going, he built a frame of green branches, sliced the venison very thin and put it to jerk just close enough to the heat so that it dried more than cooked.

They feasted that night, two men who had missed many meals in their lives, and like animals filled themselves against the days when they might starve again. Before full dark they smothered the fire and climbed the draw to the knob on which the deer had stood, where they could not be surprised.

They ate more venison steaks in the morning and Harden took the lead position. About noon the trail began to dip, then the right-hand wall lowered, disappeared, and they were on a narrow shelf angling down the side of a dropping canyon with a sheer fall of perhaps two hundred feet. The shelf was barely wider than the horse itself.

Harden's view ahead was blocked by the left wall that here jutted into a shoulder. The trail twisted around its base but he could not see where it went.

He reached the shoulder, started around it and stopped, catching his breath. A huge canyon yawned ahead and the trail sheered off completely five feet before him. He felt the horse tremble beneath him, hug the wall. He got down on the outside, awkward at the breach of habit, and worked forward, hoping the animal would not knock him off the edge in a sudden lurch.

The mule had stopped, blocking Purdy from turning the bend. Harden heard him call, 'What is it?' and looked back. Purdy, on foot, was working around the mule.

'Looks like the trail ends here.'

He cleared the horse and walked to the brink. Wherever the trail had been, it was sliced off as with a knife, leaving a vertical rock face too steep even to have caught brush or rubble.

The canyon ran both ways from them, to the

north and south. It was so deeep that it was hard to make out objects in its bottom, three, four thousand feet down or more, and the walls appeared to be sheer on both sides, making a long, sunken valley.

In the sunlight dark-green foliage covered the floor and through it a glint showed that had to be water—a river, perhaps a fork of the Yaqui.

Several miles north, on the far side of the river, was a tiny white spot with rectangular lines that could only be a building. Something stirred in Harden. Was this Tayopa?

Purdy seemed to read his mind. 'If that's it, you ain't never going to get down there.'

Harden turned back and examined the shelf they were on. The familiar marks were there, worn by burrow hoofs in times past. Obviously the trail had once continued on down into the canyon. Just as obviously something had broken loose a landslide at this fault, whether a natural earthquake or a possible deliberate explosion there was no way to say.

'We'll have to find another trail.'

Purdy looked at the sheer wall above them, the drop below. 'You're not going to find anything real close. Chances are this was the only road there was.'

Harden's head came up quickly and he sniffed the air. There was a familiar taint to it that made his eyes narrow. 'You smell what I smell?'

Purdy, testing it, look a long time to answer. 'Wood smoke.'

'Yeah.'

'Real faint. Maybe somebody's camped behind us. Maybe Indians.'

'I don't think so. There's an updraft here, out of the canyon. My guess is, there's a fire down there somewhere. That ought to mean people. And if there are people there has to be a way to get down.'

It was a delicate business, backing the animals on the narrow shelf, especially the mule. The pack bumping against the wall made its rear feet continually veer toward the edge. Purdy, at his horse's head, cajoled and shoved and finally got the frightened mount back into the cut. Then he came to help with the mule. It took the two of them to maneuver the burdened animal into the walled safety: then they continued the awkward backing to a place wide enough to turn. Afterward they retreated to where the trail had forked and took the arm that wound back eastward.

For three days they worked through rough country without finding another branch. On the fourth they came on an *Indio* woman sitting beside the trail.

She was the only human they had seen. She did not get up, but crouched away, her black eyes round on them.

Harden spoke to her in Spanish. For answer she wrapped her arms around her middle, bent forward and moaned. Harden cocked an eye at Purdy.

'What the hell's that supposed to mean?'

'I'd guess,' the black man said in a soft tone, 'that she's about ready to have a baby.'

'A baby? Here?'

The place was arid, bleak, covered with chaparral. There was no sign of a house, a hut, even a cave. Harden's Spanish was not good and he knew none of the Indian dialects at all.

'What do we do?'

'We help her.' Purdy was unhurriedly swinging out of the saddle.

Harden was sarcastic. 'And just how do we do that?'

'Get a fire going. Put what water we've got to boil. Then ride back to that seep spring we passed an hour or so ago and bring all you can.'

Dave Harden followed the orders without question, too flustered even for wonder. The seep spring was small and filling the canteens was slow. He sweated with impatience and used his horse hard in getting back.

When he did come back the woman was lying limp and still on a blanket Purdy had spread in the lacy shade of a bush and the big man was at the fire, kneeling, holding what looked like a skinned rabbit by the heels in one hand, the forefinger of his other hand probing into the tiny mouth. He twisted the finger, brought out mucous, wiped the mouth out

44

further with the sleeve of a shirt from his bedroll, then gave the ridiculously small buttocks a smart slap with a hand almost bigger than the baby. There was a thin wail, and Purdy wrapped the little body in the shirt.

Harden got down gingerly, staring from Purdy's swift, gentle hands to the quiet woman. He whispered, 'She all right? She's not dead?'

Purdy was too busy to look up. 'She had a time. Guess maybe it's her first. She's not very old even if she looks it now.'

Harden found his hands trembling as he brought the canteens. 'How'd you know what to do?'

Purdy's teeth showed in a grin then as he dipped the sleeve into the boiling water, swung it around in the air to cool it, and mopped at the wizened head.

'My ma was a midwife. I've seen a lot of children born. Never had to help myself before, but I remembered.'

Harden went to look at the new mother. Her eyes were open now, exhausted and fear-filled. He wished he could talk to her, reassure her. Then Purdy was there with his small bundle, squatting to lay it in the crook of the woman's arm, and her face changed, some of the weariness loosened into a faint smile and the fear left her eyes before she closed them. She slept at peace.

45

# CHAPTER FIVE

The Pueblo was a surprise, invisible in a high bowl surrounded by a timbered rim until they dipped into it. They had waited a day for the girl to recover, then Purdy had taken her and the baby up before him on the horse and by gestures asked where to go.

The community was bigger than Harden had expected in this country, with a decaying church facing a dusty, much trampled dirt plaza and perhaps fifty thatched huts. Excitement spread as they came into the street and short, dark, silent people erupted from the doors to stare. The hostile faces changed as they saw the girl and the child and a gabble of jabbering broke out.

Purdy swung down and reached up to take the baby in one arm, the girl in his other, and he lifted them from the saddle. A young man hurried from a house across the plaza and hungrily took the baby. A moment later an older man came from the same house, struggling into a coat. He wore a flat black hat, the wide brim trimmed with little silver bells. The coat was velvet with silver braid, a costume of the ancient hidalgo, making him a figure out of the past. He came up shooting questions at the girl and when she answered he looked at Purdy.

He spoke Spanish. 'I present myself. Don Tomás, *jefe* of the pueblo Yecroa. My son's wife tells me how you saved her. She would have been attacked by jaguars or bears, perhaps a tiger. Surely the good God sent you. We thank Him and you, Señors.' Don Tomás was a man of dignity, standing as straight as one of his ancestors' bow strings. The face was cleanly chiseled, deeply lined and his eyes had seen much hardship, much sorrow. It was in their depths even when he smiled.

Purdy made him a slight bow and rolled his eyes up at Harden, saying in a soft voice, 'Well, now we're messengers of God. Think of that.'

Harden had not known that Purdy understood Spanish. Now he learned that he also spoke it. Purdy was asking Don Tomás, 'What was she doing out there all by herself at a time like that?'

The *jefe* looked toward his son, holding the baby, one arm now around the girl's shoulders and their heads together, intent on the child, and his mouth was wry.

'She is a foolish one. She and my son argued and she set out to walk to her father's village. The baby came too soon. Now they will be wiser. You, Señors, my house is yours.' He looked up at Harden. 'If you will dismount your animals will be cared for while we talk further.'

Harden had deliberately waited for the invitation. He was uneasy here, surrounded by

47

so many of these Indians who took such a dim view of anyone hunting the old mines, and very glad that Purdy had made a friend at court. He wondered at the number of them, how they had survived the raiding Apaches and scalp hunters. Then he thought of the sardonic Apache boast that they left certain settlements alone for seed, to raise more horses and women and children for later harvesting.

At the *jefe*'s order a group of half-grown boys took over the animals and Don Tomás led Purdy and Harden to the shade of the *ramada* built beside his house. He left them and returned shortly with a skin of mescal and a clay dish holding the small, crooked cigars rolled from black native tobacco. Presently the *jefe*'s wife came, bringing a stew of boiled goat meat with tortillas. They ate ceremoniously, rolling the tortillas into cones, shoveling up the stew with them, and when they were finished Don Tomás offered more cigars.

'Now it is time for talk,' he said. 'You are looking for gold and silver in the Sierra?'

Harden had been relaxing, leaning back in the chair of woven rawhide. He snapped tense again.

'We are.' There was no use denying it, with shovel and pick lashed on the mule.

The *jefe* blew smoke, looking not at them but across the dusty plaza. 'Gold and silver . . . when they flow it is in a river of blood, Señors. They are metals of evil. When they are mined out of the earth the people are destroyed.'

Harden spoke carefully. 'When they are mined by greedy men, yes. We don't mean to mine. We're hunting for some that's already mined. If we found it we would take it away, quietly. We would bring no one back. We would not look for more. We would not speak of where it came from.'

The *jefe* reached for the mescal skin, drank from it and passed it.

'There are many dangers in the mountains.'

'There are dangers everywhere.'

Don Tomás lifted and dropped his shoulders. 'Do you have a special place to look for?'

He was in this deep, Harden thought, and he might as well go all the way. If he could not convince this village leader that he would not bring harm down on them, he was not at all sure that, in spite of Purdy's midwifing, they weren't in trouble. How far the people of Yecroa would go to keep the secrets of the Sierras he did not know. He watched the man's face.

'Tayopa,' he said. 'We have a map. Do you know of it?'

The *jefe* might have bitten into something with a bad taste. 'I know the name. In my family there was one who worked there. He could walk there from this village, and when the wind was right he could hear the bell from the church at sundown. But I do not know the direction.'

Harden met Purdy's eyes. Since they had turned back from the sheered-off trail they had moved in a wide, rough circle. He felt a fresh shiver run through him.

'Do you know an ancient ranch in a deep canyon to the west, with many trees growing along a river, and a white building?'

Don Tomás hesitated for a long while. He took another powerful pull from the mescal skin. 'I have heard of it, I have not seen it.'

'Do you know how to get there?'

The man looked at Purdy then back at Harden with outright pleading in his eyes.

'You should not try, my friends. Countrymen of yours have taken up a place on the cerro above the old road that skirts the mountain. They allow no one to pass.'

'Americans? Who are they, miners? Scalp hunters?'

Don Tomás shrugged. 'It is said they fought in your recent rebellion on the losing side.'

'Confederates?' There was a hard laugh from Purdy.

Harden had heard of southerners refusing to swear allegiance to the Union at the end of the war and retreating into Mexico and South America, but he did not know any had come as far west as the Siera Madre.

'Why won't they let people go to the canyon?'

'They are hard men. They have guns. There

has been trouble. I give you the warning because you helped us.'

'Thank you for that, Don Tomás. What's the name of the mountain?'

'The Cerro de la Campana.'

The *jefe* got up and reluctantly walked out to the street, pointed to a distant mountain with pine-covered sides rising abruptly to a flat top. Harden's practiced eye measured it as nearly a mile high above the basin.

'I think,' Purdy said softly, 'we'll have a look.'

And Don Tomás gave up his arguments.


# CHAPTER SIX

They rode out at first light with gifts of tortillas and a mescal skin in their saddlebags. The villagers lined the street, watching them go. They were neither hostile nor friendly. Rather they looked as if they were attending a funeral.

'*Vaya con Dios,*' Don Tomás said and placed his hat over his heart as if in a final salute.

The girl with the baby clung to her husband, hiding her face in his shoulder.

Riding out of the pueblo at Harden's side Purdy said, 'Must be a real tough place we're headed.'

'You don't have to go.'

The Negro looked at him, offended, and

51

Harden laughed. 'Don't get thin-skinned on me, Luke.'

'Mr. Harden.' The use of the mister showed his offense. 'A man like me can't afford a thin skin. And I do have to go. You heard what the man said. Those are southerners on the *cerro*. You know what I'm looking for.'

'I hope you find him.'

'I will.' Purdy lapsed into a tight-lipped silence.

As far as the foot of the *cerro* the trail was clear enough. It showed little travel in recent times, but the old deep-worn rocks remained. When it began to climb through scrub brush the wind helped clear leaves out of the track. Then it steepened and they were in the pines. Years of falling needles had laid a soft bed over the rock, but by watching ahead they could find a faint depression that wound upward. They lost it often, had to retrace and scout out to pick up the ghost of the ancient way again. It took them the whole day to reach the plateau top.

From below Harden had guessed the mountain to be thirty or forty miles long, but when they leveled out, the mesa was too thickly timbered to see any distance. They found signs of deer, quail, bear and mountain lions, and there was plenty of water, little streams running across the rolling flat land.

The direction of the sun told Harden that they were not following along the axis of the *cerro* but angling across it. In another day they reached the far side and turned along that. It was not an abrupt drop but a ragged area where the streams, running into each other, began to fall and through the centuries had cut a series of canyons veering down toward the plain.

The trail took them into one of these canyons, down a zigzag of switchbacks as the slope steepened. The stream here grew, and fed by side rivulets, became a good-sized river that Harden was sure must be one of the forks of the Yaqui. The canyon opened out at a wide bench halfway down the *cerro* side, and river and trail turned to follow that. As they lost altitude the character of the vegetation changed. The pines were left above and they traveled through thick clumps of madroño trees. Birds, quail especially, were abundant. Parrots squawked from the brush and jays cried their anger.

The trail wound past the mouths of several steep canyons that ran up on their right side, bent around the blunt nose of one intervening ridge, and intersected a road that climbed a canyon that appeared no different from the others.

But here the intersecting road was framed by an arch. Cedar posts set on either side supported a crossbar with a legend burned into it: RANCHO DE TAYOPA.

Dave Harden stared, unbelieving. Cedar

lasted a long time in that country, but these posts had not stood there for more than ten years at most, to judge by their solid condition.

The road under them and the trail that continued to follow the bench beyond showed recent travel, prints in the dust of mules, shod horses and some kind of wheeled vehicle.

Harden turned to look at Purdy. The sometime-sergeant was studying the prints with thoughtful eyes, saying softly, 'Seems like there's been a lot of coming and going.'

'Yeah.'

Purdy lifted his attention to the legend burned in the bar. 'Looks like we found that lost mine of yours.'

'Maybe.'

'What's *maybe* mean?'

'Lots of other people have heard of Tayopa, Luke. Could be if I was going to start a ranch around here I'd think it was kind of cute to name it that.'

'Could be.'

'Whichever it is, I've come a lot of hard miles to find Tayopa. Be a shame to come this close and not have a look. What do you think?'

'Think maybe you're right. We might find some southerners up that hill.' Purdy heeled his horse and walked it under the arch.

The canyon climbed gently, twisting up the course that the clear-running stream in its bed had worn. They followed it up for some five miles, then it pinched in between sheer rock dikes that rose a hundred feet. Beyond the dikes a breathtaking view spread before them. Here was a great bowl of a valley where there might once have been a lake damned up by the dikes before they were cut apart, set deep back into the flank of the *cerro* and half a mile below the mesa top.

The valley floor was rich and green with grass, a natural pasture enclosed palisades as steep but not as high as the walls of the canyon that might be Tayopa. Cattle could not possibly climb out of it. A man could not.

Harden judged the valley to be near five miles across and twice that deep, and it was peppered with fat cattle peacefully grazing across the deep carpet of red-stemmed grass. There was no question that it was a ranch, and one that any man would dream of.

They sat their horses a long time, drinking in the sight, then Purdy let his breath out in a long sigh.

'My, oh my. Did you ever see anything prettier, Dave?'

'I never did.' Harden urged his horse forward. 'Let's go have a closer look.'

The road ran straight, a ranch lane toward the upper end of the valley, and at its end they began to make out a cluster of log buildings, with smoke rising from stovepipes.

The large yard was fenced to keep the loose stock away from the buildings with a wide gate closing the lane. Purdy swung down to open the gate. He had barely touched it when a man stepped suddenly around a clump of bushes on the inside.

'Keep your hands off of that, nigra.'

Purdy froze. A quick, hot anger burned through Harden. It was not so much the word—he had heard it applied to black men many times. It was the tone that sparked the rage. The man carried a Winchester loosely in big red hands. Harden could not tell whether that was their natural color or if they burned instead of tanning in the sun. He shifted slightly in the saddle to free his gun hand, quartered from the man watching Purdy.

Dave said quietly, 'Just put that rifle down.'

The man was tall, heavy-shouldered, thick-bodied, his big head set like a bull's on a short neck. He turned the head and his little eyes flicked as he saw the muzzle of Dave's hand gun peeping at him over the high horn of the Texas saddle.

Harden could see him think. The man could not swing the rifle around before Dave could squeeze the Colt's trigger. He knew it and he knew something else. Purdy's shoulders had shifted as Dave spoke. If he swung the rifle to cover Dave Purdy would probably shoot him in the side. He was nicely boxed, and the knowledge sparked a fury in him. His harsh voice came out strangled.

'You'll be sorry. You'll be sorry. You ride out of here while you can.'

'Drop the gun.'

'You'll be sorry.'

'You said that.' Dave's tone was flat, final. 'I won't tell you again. I can blow out your liver.'

The rifle dropped, hardly making a sound as it hit the grass matting.

'Now open the gate.'

The man's mouth dropped, like a gasping fish. Dave was afraid he would say 'You'll be sorry' again. But he walked to the gate, stretched the red hands out to unlatch it and swung it wide.

'Now,' Dave said, 'walk ahead of us. Take us to your boss.'

The little eyes glared. 'I gotta shut the gate.'

'Purdy, bring the mule and shut the gate after you.'

Harden rode through as the man threw himself around and strode up the yard toward the biggest of four buildings.

The man wore a gun belt and holstered weapon but Harden dropped his own Colt back into its place. He felt confident that he could pull it and fire before the man could turn and shoot, and he thought it bad policy to ride in on this strange ranch with a gun in his hand. He already regretted the impulse that had made him draw rather than try to talk the man down.

The house they approached was unusual in that it was made of logs in this country where all major structures were either stone or adobe. It was built Texas-style, two independent units connected by a covered breezeway.

The big man stopped in front of the porch and yelled an unintelligible word. After a moment Harden stopped being interested in the man as a woman came from the door on the right.

She was dressed in black, after the fashion of the Spanish hacienda women: black pants, black bolero over a white blouse and a flat-crowned black hat. Her hair was light, a yellow-gold, fastened in a knot at the nape of her neck so that the hat sat over it. She wore black gloves and black boots of soft leather. She carried a rifle as if she were familiar with it.

The last thing Harden had expected to find in this vast isolation was an American woman, particularly so beautiful a woman as this. She looked to be in her mid-thirties, thirty-five at most, and the eyes she leveled on him were a light, cold gray, imperious as her thin-walled nose with the up-flaring nostrils. There was no softness in them nor in the delicate, patrician face.

She ignored the man who had stopped them at the gate, walked by him, her eyes taking in Purdy's silent bulk, moving past him to rivet on Dave Harden. Her voice was low, controlled, with no note of feeling.

'What do you want here?'

Harden took off his hat, held it in his lap and matched her tone.

'I saw the name of the ranch on your arch. I was curious.'

'Why?'

'Tayopa. I'm looking for a lost mine called Tayopa. I wondered why you chose it.'

The careful eyes went over him, taking in the worn, stained clothes, the pack mule, Purdy's straight-backed figure.

'My brother chose it.' The words still had no inflection. 'I never asked him why.'

Harden eased himself in the saddle. Her hold on the rifle had not relaxed and from the corner of his eye he saw the guard shift to one side so that she no longer stood between them. Harden tried smiling.

'I'd like to ask your brother about his reason.'

'That will not be possible. He has been dead for six months.'

'Oh.' Harden did not know quite what to say, how to offer sympathy to this icy woman. 'Then if I could talk to whoever is running the ranch?'

'I am.'

They watched each other warily. Although the woman appeared calm, poised, Harden sensed that underneath she was nervous. He tried to reassure her.

'I'm Dave Harden,' he said. 'An old Mexican gave me a map that he claims shows the

59

location of the ancient mines of Tayopa . . . '

'There are no mines here. I am afraid you have come on a wild-goose chase.'

He widened his smile. 'Anyone who hunts lost mines or buried treasures is used to wild-goose chases. But we've come a long way. Will it be all right if we camp down in the pasture for a day or two . . . to rest the animals?'

This time she did not bite him off, did not answer immediately. He read her mind that she wanted them gone and was debating the best way to get rid of them. The attitude added to the growing puzzle. What was a woman like this doing here? Why had her brother used the name Tayopa and not explained it to her? Or did she know, and know where the mines were . . . ?

Then she spoke, as if to herself. 'If I refuse you permission you'll probably only ride out beyond the dikes and stay there.'

'That's right. The horses are tired.'

'Very well, have your man make your camp beside the creek, down the valley. I must ask you not to come near the buildings again.'

His man . . . He glanced around, met Purdy's eyes and saw the lips twitch as if to control a smile, then he turned back.

'Thank you, Ma'am.'

He put his hat on, swung his horse and winked at Purdy. They rode back to where the stream cut across the meadow and chose a spot where a stand of timber made an island in the grass. There they took the pack off the mule and unsaddled and picketed the horses.

Harden, watching behind as he rode, had seen the man who had stopped them stand talking to the woman. The next time he looked the man was at the corral saddling a horse. As they reached their campsite the man had mounted. He rode to the gate and got down to pick up the rifle he had dropped there. He opened the gate, led his horse through and fastened the gate behind him. Then he remounted and rode down the long lane and out of sight.

The woman too had gone to the corral. She brought out a big chestnut, saddled it expertly, swung up and drove it at a gallop around the buildings, into the timber at the head of the valley.

There was no one else in sight in the big pasture.

Purdy had not spoken since they had ridden in. He made a fire, went to the creek for fresh water and put it to heat. Harden unpacked the cooking gear and stood above Purdy.

'What do you think, Luke?'

The big shoulders moved. Purdy did not look up. 'What's to think?'

'Have these people found the Tayopa treasure?'

'Can't say. They weren't right pleased to see us, but that you can understand.'

'What do you mean?'

Purdy sat back on his heels and let the twisted smile come. 'Well, sir, from her talk I'd say that lady came from Texas or somewhere along the Mississippi. Her folks lost a war, and they ran, and now a black man comes riding big into their yard.'

'That doesn't hurt them.'

'No, it don't hurt them, but look at it their way. They lost and my people won, as it were. Then, too, I'm still wearing a uniform, and it's blue. Makes it a double insult, don't you see.'

'I suppose so.' Harden had not thought of it in quite that light. 'I wonder where the fellow went, down the valley.'

'And where the lady went. Could be they're out to round up some help to get rid of us.'

Harden poured the boiling water into the coffee pot. 'I think we both want to wait around and see.'

## CHAPTER SEVEN

The boy came riding toward them, a very small boy looking even smaller on the back of the horse. Neither of them knew exactly where he had come from. Suddenly he was loping across the grass toward the fire.

Harden stood up to greet him. 'Hello, there.'

The boy nodded soberly but his eyes were

lively. He was six or seven, not older. His head was bare, his yellow hair cut short, and freckles crossed his turned-up nose and spread over both cheeks. His voice was light and openly curious.

'Who are you? Where'd you come from?'

Harden grinned. His grin could be infectious and the boy's delicate lips turned up.

'My name's Dave Harden and I came down from Arizona.' He tipped his head toward Purdy, still squatted by the fire. 'That's Luke Purdy. He's from Arizona too.'

The boy took in the faded uniform. 'You in the army?'

Purdy stood up but did not move toward the horse. 'I was, for a time.'

'My paw was in the army too. He was a colonel before the damn yankees whipped us.'

'Do tell.' Purdy sounded impressed.

'If you don't believe it you can ask my maw or my aunt.'

Harden said, 'Where's your daddy now?'

'In heaven.' The boy pointed at the sky. 'A snake bit him.'

'I'm sorry. Who's taking care of the ranch?'

'My aunt Ethel and my mother.'

'They've got to have some help.'

'Oh, sure. Mr. Sands is foreman and we got four other riders. We had twelve more only they went back to Texas to get recruits.'

Harden and Purdy looked at each other.

63

'Recruits for what?'

The boy's eyes danced, thoroughly enjoying having this new audience.

'We're going to start a new country here. A country the damnyankees and the niggers can't take away from us.'

His eyes widened on Purdy. Apparently it had just dawned on him that Purdy's skin was black.

'You're a nigger.'

Purdy didn't say anything. Harden changed the subject.

'So you're going to start a new country. That costs a lot of money.'

The boy sounded eager, excited. 'Oh, we got plenty of money. We got the treasure.'

Purdy coughed. Harden did not look his way, but nodded to the boy.

'The Tayopa treasure, and the ranch is named for it?'

The boy was pleased that they shared a knowledge, but he wanted to stay one up.

'Well, Paw named the ranch after the old town in the canyon.'

'And he found the silver under the church.'

Now a hint of nervousness sobered the boy as if he suddenly realized that he had said too much.

'He found it, but it ain't there now.'

'You mean he moved it?'

'I ain't supposed to tell . . .'

Harden did not press him. He smiled again.

64

'You didn't give us your name.'

The voice was relieved that they had been thrown off the track. 'It's Tommy Mayfield. It was my father's name too, and my grandfather's and my great-grandfather's. He fought in the Revolution.'

'Just think of that,' Purdy said solemnly.

'I gotta go,' Tommy said abruptly. 'I got chores to do.' He started to turn the horse, then he blurted, 'You won't try to find the silver, will you? Sands kills anybody that tries.' He did not wait for the answer, but kicked his heels against the horse's flanks and galloped away.

Harden watched him go, saying over his shoulder, 'That canyon we looked down into, that must be where Tayopa was. Shall we go take a look?'

Purdy dumped the coffee on the fire, killing it.

They loaded the mule again, saddled and rode out. If anyone in the buildings watched them they gave no sign. The bowl valley looked empty of life except for the fat cattle and horses in the dusty corral.

They hit the bench trail near midday and turned west along it. The trail worsened rapidly and when they passed the west end of the great butte the country became a badlands of deep, dry arroyos and rearing ridges. Darkness caught them in the third arroyo. They used the canteens sparingly, picketed the

65

animals and climbed to sleep among the cluster of rock bursts up the steep side.

Before the sun was high enough to light their camp they rode again, up onto a low mesa whose crown was eroded with a series of many gashes. There were no trees as far as they could see from its top. The trail zigzagged across the mesa on a crooked westerly course, dipping into the ragged cuts, rising out of them on tight switchbacks. They did not reach the far side of it until late afternoon, then they turned a shoulder and were at the rim, with a broad view of what lay below.

It could only be the canyon they had seen where the other trail was sheered off, and still a mile deep. This point was north of the other and the white building much closer, a square tower at one end of it indicating a church. Harden felt the pulse, the heady tingling through his body that is the wine of all prospectors when they make a strike. It made no difference to him that the silver was gone. Psychologically he had set out to find the lost mines of Tayopa. He had found Tayopa.

The trail turned down on a narrow shelf against the face of the wall. The rim edge was crooked as though the mesa had been cut off by a giant scalloped blade and the face plunged directly down. From where they sat they could pick out sections of the slanting trail following the scallops on a steep angle so that they were broken into falling, disconnected stretches with the lowest one, which would meet the valley floor, among those that were not in sight.

Luke Purdy looked at the ball of the sun sitting on the western rim of the canyon and said, 'It's gonna be dark before we could get halfway down there, Dave. Me, I vote we make another dry camp up here and wait for morning.'

Harden was impatient but he was not an imprudent man. 'I guess it's not going to run away,' he said, and they moved back from the rim.

The wisdom of waiting was proved the next day. The shelf was seldom wide enough to turn a horse, seldom had any protecting rise of rock on the outside. Most of the way it was a dizzying precipice. One misstep would send a horse and rider off in a straight drop.

Dave Harden was very glad to make that last turn and see ahead the end of the trail. It went through a man-made cut sliced through a high wedge of broken rock that had fallen out of the rim and blocked the trail with a mound that ran down from the wall to the edge of the river. Once beyond that they angled down the rubble slope to where a tongue of it made a shallow ford across the river.

Except for the bare rock slide the floor was covered with trees. The trail wound under them and across small, grassy glades. Half a mile west of the river was an opening of brush and grass. And there was the church. It was large, built of squared stone, coated with thick whitewash only partly peeled. The roof of both the bell tower and the main building were caved in; the red tiles had fallen in and the interior was open to the sky. A grove of trees had grown up within the walls. Lush grass beneath them made it look like a little park.

The mud huts of the Indian slaves had melted without a trace under a mesh of brush, but behind the church the old orchard, gone wild, still bore fruit. They rode among the trees—orange, pomegranate, peach, quince, banana and other varieties that Harden could not identify—all fighting for space among the encroachment of native growth. There was much animal sign from deer, jaguar and panther, and fat quail ran away from them in flocks.

Purdy shot several of the birds with his revolver. It was no great trick, for they ran only a few feet and then ostrichlike buried their heads in the grass.

'Man, oh man,' he gloated. 'If this don't beat the garden of Eden. All the fruit a man could eat . . . all the meat . . . and I'll bet you could grow anything else you wanted like you never saw. It's real queer none of the *indios* have taken up this place. I wonder why.'

'It's a place of the dead,' Harden said. 'Apaches massacred all the slaves after the priests left. You couldn't get an Indian to live

68

here to save his life.'

Purdy was already pulling the feathers off the birds, almost smacking his lips. Harden turned away to hide his grin, picketed the animals, then went to the church.

The strap hinges on the heavy doors had rusted and the panels had fallen in and rotted. Dave stood at the entrance with his pocket compass and found that the structure faced due east. He got out the translation of his map, read the directions, and began a wide circle of the building, pacing off a thousand yards. That took him to a small hill and on a hunch he dug into it, found as he suspected that it was an old dump of slag. From there he searched for the vaso in which the ore had been smelted and located it at some distance from the dump. But he had not yet come upon any mine.

When he did he nearly fell into it, a depression not six feet across. The mouth of the shaft had been floored over with logs and those covered with dirt to disguise it. In the years since, the logs had rotted and his weight cracked one of them. He sank through knee-deep before he threw himself flat, backward, to keep from dropping through entirely, worked his leg free and went back to the camp for his shovel.

'I found one mine,' he told Purdy. 'They were gopher-holing. You want to look?'

'It won't go away,' Purdy said. 'Let's eat. These birds are just right now.'

He had laid out a feast of ripe fruit, cold tortillas and quail roasted on spits of green sticks. Harden ate hurriedly, impatient, to Purdy's great disapproval, and the black man was reaching for a third bird when Harden got up, picked up his tools and started for the mine. Purdy wagged his head, sighed, and followed, gnawing at the quail as he went.

He stood by as Harden shoveled the dirt from the logs, then used his pick to break some of the rotted wood away and partly open the shaft.

Water stood just below the logs, filling the shaft. Harden rolled a large stone into it and listened closely, hoping to hear it hit bottom, to judge the depth. No sound came back.

'Well,' Purdy wiped his hands on his trousers. 'We're not going to dig any silver out of there. What do we do now?'

'Hunt for some others. There were supposed to be seventeen around here.'

Purdy found four by the time Harden located the entrance to the treasure tunnel. Either the translation of the instructions was wrong or his compass was, for there was nothing at the point indicated. Again the discovery was accidental.

Purdy had found a fifth depression and called him. Dave started toward him, pushing through deep brush, and suddenly he was standing at the edge of an open, dry hole. Beside it was a pile of dirt with no grass on it, and scattered chunks of rotted logs.

He stood looking down into the dark depth and his voice shook with excitement, calling, 'Purdy, find some pitch wood. Bring some knots for torches.'

It was not that he expected to find silver left in the tunnel. If the little boy had told the truth, which he saw no reason to doubt, the treasure had been moved. It was the fact that the map had been right, had led him to this spot that had him trembling. That finding wealth is the goal of the prospector is only the lesser half of truth. The thing that sends him out and keeps him going is the search itself and the proving of his faith in his judgment

Purdy came with an armload of knots so filled with pitch that Harden lit one with a match. Taking that and a long branch with which to beat for snakes, he gingerly started down the flight of stone steps. The bottom was only ten feet deep and from it a tunnel led toward the church. He called Purdy to join him and walked into the tunnel, studying it in the unsteady torch light.

The walls were cut stone so cunningly fit together that no mortar had been needed. The roof arched so that he could nearly stand erect. The floor slanted down gently and was cushioned with thick dust. Beating at the walls and the arch, sweeping the floor ahead as he went, he was surprised to find no snakes.

The tunnel finally opened into a room ten

feet square with a vaulted roof. Around the stone walls sat long, wooden seats. While Purdy held the torches Harden started at the nearest and opened them all. Most were empty. There was a single silver cross in one and in the last were parchment scrolls.

Harden felt his heart pound against his ribs as he lifted one out, unrolled it. He knew that he held one of the once precious records of the hacienda of Tayopa. The writings were too faded to make out in the smoky torch light but there could be no doubt. They were inside the treasure house of the ancient town.

Purdy turned about, looking at the empty chest. 'All gone.' He sounded breathless. 'All gone. How much was there supposed to be, Dave?'

'Thirty million pesos.'

'Thirty million is a lot of anything. Think how close you and I came to having all of that ourselves.'

Harden, putting the parchment back, could not resist saying, 'I thought you weren't interested in the money?'

Purdy grinned sheepishly. 'That's what I said, and that's what I meant. But I'd like just to have seen it once. There aren't many men ever saw that kind of money, now are there?'

'Mighty few, Luke.'

'Suppose we was to find where those folks up on that mountain hid it. What then?'

Harden straightened to meet the other's

eyes. There was a silent moment, then Harden said thoughtfully, 'I don't know, Luke. I honestly don't know. They say every man has a price. I never yet found out what my price would be.'

'Pretty big decision to make, isn't it?'

Harden reached for one of the torches. 'Let's go get some more quail, or maybe a deer. This is a nice place to stay for a few days while we think about it.'

The Negro started to say something else, then changed his mind. He turned away and led off, back out of the passage.


## CHAPTER EIGHT

There was no warning. Purdy climbed out of the shaft and stood at the edge, watching Harden come up. They dropped the torches to burn out on the floor below. And four men were out of the brush, against them.

A gun barrel crashed down on top of Purdy's campaign hat. He fell without a sound and lay still.

Harden's right hand made a convulsive move for his belt gun. Before he touched it a rifle barrel was rammed into his stomach, driving the wind out of him. He gasped, strangling, trying to catch his breath.

A big man with sunburned yellow hair and

tight blue eyes said, 'Fenner, drag the nigra over to the horses.'

'Glad to, Sands.' The man who had stopped them at the ranch gate caught Purdy's feet, heaved, grunting as he tried to pull Purdy's heavy body.

'Give me a hand, Bell.'

A short, squat man with a knife scar on his cheek took one foot; Fenner kept the other. Between them they dragged the limp figure through the bushes.

Sands spoke to Harden. 'You couldn't keep your nose out of this canyon, huh? Miss Ethel figured so.'

Harden said flatly, 'What gives you the right to say I can't come here?'

'This does.' Sands tapped the rifle lightly. 'You want to argue?'

Harden did not. There was no chance against four heavily armed men. Sands read the message in his face.

'Sutliff, get his gun.'

Sutliff, little more than a boy, stepped in and lifted Harden's Colt from the holster.

'Now, you, walk over to the horses.'

Harden pushed through the brush the way Purdy had been dragged. Purdy lay on his back, his eyes closed. Sutliff brought a bucket of water from the river and threw it full into Purdy's face. Purdy stirred and groaned. Fenner came to stand above him.

'Come on, nigra, on your feet.' He kicked

74

Purdy in the side, hard, twice. 'That's for being black and wearing that damn uniform.'

Harden made no move. There was nothing he could do. His initial flare of hot anger had passed and left him with a cold, dangerous fury.

He sensed Sands watching him, the thin lips twisted in sardonic amusement as if this was a welcome break in the monotony of running the isolated ranch.

Purdy groaned again. A second bucket of water was dashed in his face and he shook his head groggily, sat up, then slowly got to his feet and stood unsteadily. His brown eyes looked dull but Harden read murder in their depths.

Sands said, 'Sutliff, bring their horses, tie the mule to one of them. Bell, you lead out. You two, follow Bell on foot.'

Harden found the reins of his horse shoved into his hand. Someone he could not see threw a saddle on the animal and Sutliff tied the mule's lead rope to the horn. At Sands' order Harden began walking, following Bell and Purdy.

Fenner rode on ahead alone. Harden heard a shot up that way and when they came near the river Fenner was gutting a doe. It was thrown across Purdy's horse and tied there, then they crossed the ford.

The walk up the shelf trail was hard going, but Harden preferred that to riding in this

75

company. It would be too easy for one of these men to jab a horse, startle it into a jump that would pitch him into the abyss.

It was dusk when they reached the top and a camp was made there, the fresh-killed deer butchered and roasted. The riders hobbled their horses at a distance and spread their bedrolls. Harden and Purdy were ignored, and sank down gratefully. They were unarmed and even if they could reach the horses a rifle could pick them off easily.

No one was with them but Purdy kept his voice low. 'Do you make any sense of this?'

'Not much,' Harden admitted. 'If they mean to kill us why haven't they done it already?'

'I've been wondering. I don't like the way Fenner looks at me. Don't like that heavy boot of his. That kicking hurt. Maybe it busted one of my ribs.'

'I don't see what we can do about it, do you?'

Purdy shook his head. 'I don't mind dying— man's got to die sometime—but I hate to come this close and not be able to finish what I came for.'

Harden was watching the men around the fire. He said without turning his head, 'Think one of these is the man you're looking for?'

'Seems likely. They fought for the South so a slave catcher would naturally feel at home with them.'

'Which one?'

'Can't tell. No, I can't rightly tell, but I'll bet on Fenner. He hates me because I'm black.'

They stopped talking as Sands brought plates of meat to them, dropped a canteen of water between them.

'Eat up, then I'll tie you for the night. Can't have you wandering off in the dark and falling off the edge.'

In the morning they were routed out early, fed and permitted to ride, only, Sands said, in the interest of time. It was full dark when they passed the dikes guarding the ranch entrance and saw the distant glow of the windows of the Rancho de Tayopa's main house.

Sands sent Purdy under Fenner's guard to the tool shed and prodded Harden up onto the breezeway and through the door into the living room. A fire blazed in a big-throated fireplace and Ethel Mayfield stood in front of it.

Sands said with deep satisfaction, 'Well, here he is. They found the tunnel all right, just like you guessed.'

She still wore the black costume, but without hat or gloves, and the fire sparked golden highlights in her hair. In spite of her being older than he, in spite of her cold bearing she was the most beautiful woman Harden had ever seen. He had little to compare her by. There were few women of any kind in the country prospectors prowled, and those in the saloons were nothing to remember. She lifted her head imperiously.

'Come here, Harden.'

He left Sands standing at the door, the man's fingers resting lightly on his gun, and walked to the woman. She raised a hand to stop him six feet from her.

'Who are you spying for?'

He started, then in spite of himself he grinned. 'Nobody, Ma'am.'

'I think you are. I think one of our recruiters was either careless in his talk or sold us out. I think the damn carpetbaggers who took over Texas sent you and that nigra down here to take our treasure. And I'll get the truth.'

From the glint in her eyes he knew that he and Purdy were in mortal danger. They were still alive only to be questioned, under torture if need be, unless he could satisfy this woman as to why he had come.

'Nobody sent me.' He was as earnest as he knew how to be. 'I'm a prospector and always have been. I did a favor for an old Mexican and he gave me a map . . . ' He dug in his pocket. 'This one. The way to Tayopa. I followed it, I didn't know anything about anyone being here.'

She did not touch it, waved it aside. 'You found it in the box under the church. There were a lot of parchments there.'

'If I had done that would I have had time to make this translation? I can't even read old Spanish.'

She hesitated, then shook her head as if to

shake off doubt, but she changed her tactics.

'It is very important for me to know the truth. Listen. I'll tell you why.' There was an intensity in her tone that had a physical force. 'My brother was down here after the War. He heard about Tayopa and found this valley for a ranch, then he came home and gathered a herd of wild cattle and drove them down here. He brought me, his wife and son and seventeen men. To start a new state, a new nation.'

It was not unbelievable to Harden. Filibusterers had been trying to grab parts of Mexico and Central America ever since the gold rush to California.

'We expected to build gradually, increase the cattle until they could support more men, and hunt for the Tayopa silver. When we finally found that we didn't have to wait to expand.'

She had begun to move, pacing like a caged cat back and forth before him, arms tightly folded under her breasts, her voice raising and turning shrill.

'We didn't have to wait any longer. We could have our country within a year. My brother sent twelve men north as recruiters. We wanted married men, men with families, enough of them to hold our country against the Mexicans, against the Americans, against everybody.'

She all but screamed the word, flinging out

an arm in an all-encompassing sweep. Across her shoulder he saw a flag enshrined in a bay in the far wall, the stars and bars on a broken staff, the folds tattered by bullet holes. The Confederacy still lived in this room, and so did madness. She was breathing heavily, her eyes blazing at him and her tone dropped to an ominous threat.

'I know one of those twelve men we sent up to Texas told about the treasure. I warned the Colonel that someone would and he laughed at me. They had been with him all through the War and he was fool enough to think they were all as loyal as he.' She stabbed an arm at him. 'Which one? Name me the man who told you and I'll give you five thousand pesos of silver.'

'No one told me anything.'

For an instant he thought she would claw him, then she stepped back and looked to Sands.

'Tie him with the nigra in the storeroom. In the morning string him up by the thumbs and if that doesn't change his song use your whip. Cut him into jerky.'

Sands had his gun in his hand. He motioned with it toward the door. Harden went toward it, glancing back once at the woman. Her face was as expressionless as a marble statue.

The tool and storeroom was a log building over twenty-five feet long, filled with barrels of flour, bags of beans, strings of dried meat, extra saddles, bridles, tools, clothing, goods of all kinds.

Luke Purdy sat in an empty spot. His wrists were tied together under his raised knees. His ankles were bound. A noose around his neck depended from a roof beam, the rope so taut that he could not bend forward without choking.

Harden stumbled as Sands shoved him through the door, then followed, bringing a lighted lantern that hung outside. Dave caught himself, saw Purdy and swung around, regardless of Sands' gun.

'Take that rope off his neck.'

Sands' lips thinned back. 'Why?'

'For God's sake.' Harden had never been so furious. 'I wouldn't do that to a lobo wolf. Take the rope off. He can't move anywhere the way he's trussed.'

Sands' faint smile did not change. 'That Fenner, he doesn't like nigras.' He jerked his thumb. 'Go sit down by him.'

Dave Harden had had enough. He walked to Purdy, reached up, untied the rope at the beam, spread the loop and lifted it over Purdy's head. Purdy's lips moved in thanks, without sound as Harden threw the rope away from him. Then Dave turned around, expecting a rush or a shot, but Sands had not moved, was still smiling.

'Feel better? Now do like I said. Sit down. Tie your ankles together.'

The gun moved suggestively. Sands would

81

not kill him now, Dave thought, but he might well wound him, knock him out. He sat down and tied his ankles.

'Now reach under your knees and cross your wrists.'

Again Dave obeyed. Sands held his gun leveled close to Purdy's face, ready to fire if Harden tried a move. With his free hand he slipped a loop over Dave's wrists and jerked it tight, knotted it and wrapped the rope end around Dave's ankles for good measure. Then he stood back.

'You want some advice?'

Neither of them answered.

'Tell Miss Ethel everything she wants to know. It's the only chance you've got.'

He went out then and they heard him fasten the door from the outside. Without the lantern Harden could not see Purdy now but the man's breathing was ragged, gasping to fill his starved lungs.

'You all right?'

'Depends on what you call all right. I didn't expect to see you again. It makes me feel better.'

'Don't get carried away. They'll kill us both in the morning.'

'What's so important about us?'

'They've found a fortune, Luke. If word of it gets out every saddle bum along the border will be after it and the Mexican government will claim it as treasure trove. They're not strong enough here to hold it, and that woman knows it.'

'Then why are we still alive?'

'She thinks one of the riders they sent back to Texas talked. She wants to know which one and who he told the story to.'

'And she thinks we know.'

'Yeah. I couldn't convince her different.'

Purdy sucked in a long breath. 'Well, Dave, it was nice I knew you. You're about the decentest white man I ever met.'

They fell silent, found nothing more to say. The prospect of certain death in the morning was frightening. Dave had brushed death many times but had always believed he could survive. He allowed himself no illusion about Ethel Mayfield. She had dedicated herself to her brother's dream of building a replacement for the lost Confederacy and she was a bigot. He was more afraid of bigots than anything he had faced.

He did not think he had slept until noise waked him. He started up and sat tense, listening for it to come again. When it did it was at the door, someone working with the latch. Then a strip of gray night, lighter than the dense dark inside, widened, a shadow blocked it for a moment, then it narrowed to nothing. A brief breath of fresh air touched his face.

He thought it was Sands or Fenner checking on them. Then a match flared, a candle was lit and the yellow glow spread up onto a woman's head. It was not Ethel Mayfield.

She crossed the room hurriedly, a slight figure in pants and close-fitted jacket with soft brown hair falling around her shoulders. Her eyes were brown in the candle light and her speech was soft with the slur of the Gulf country.

She looked from one to the other as they watched her. 'If I turn you loose will you promise never to tell a soul about us being here, or about the treasure, or Ethel's plans?'

Harden was too surprised to answer but Purdy said fervently, 'We sure do.'

She kept her attention on Harden. 'I'm risking a lot, possibly even my son's life. I don't know you. I have to trust you. But there's been too much killing. I can't stand any more.'

Harden, said, 'My honor on it. We won't betray you.'

She seemed almost not to care, pulling a knife out of her shirt front, slashing at the rope around his ankles, then his wrists, turning at once to Purdy. It struck Harden that this might be a trap, that they were being set up for murder by someone opposed to Ethel, possibly Fenner.

Then she was saying, 'Your horses are saddled, in the corral. The guard is full of mescal, asleep.'

As she started backing away Harden said, 'Guns?'

'No guns. You might try to capture the ranch. Just be thankful for the chance I give you and go.'

She backed to the door then, felt for its handle, blew out the candle and went through leaving the door wide. Harden was right behind her, Purdy at his heels.

Outside, the moon was paling. It was almost morning. They ran to the corral and found the horses tied to the top rail as promised. Purdy loosened his and swung up. The mule was still loose in the enclosure and Harden abandoned it, but the pack was lying by the gate where it had been tossed. He ran to it, filled his pockets with tortillas and jerked meat, then as an afterthought he caught up the sack of dynamite and the coil of fuse, and sprinted back to his horse. Since they had no guns the dynamite might come in handy. He did not know exactly how, but it was little enough added burden.

Purdy had Dave's horse untied and he swung up, reined it around and they rode out.

## CHAPTER NINE

It was hard to resist bolting, but they walked the horses out of the yard and passed through the gate, making no sound on the deep mat of grass. Night was already fading from the eastern sky. They would not have too much start before the ranch people roused.

But there was hope. If they could get clear of the valley before sunup Harden doubted that any pursuit would catch them. If they could make the pueblo of Yecroa, get corn and meat there, if their luck held they could work across the mountains to Chihuahua.

Then, just as he started to knee his horse into a run, Purdy pulled up sharply and pointed.

'Apaches.'

Against the sweep of the meadow he saw them, dark shapes pouring up past the dikes, and the thin, high, yelping cry carried to him. A rifle cracked in the quiet morning air.

He swung his horse with Purdy. It was noticeably lighter. He could make out the ranch buildings clearly. They drove toward them. There was no place else to go.

Harden twisted in his saddle as his horse ran. The Indians were a quarter of a mile behind, and there were a lot of them, thirty or forty at a rough guess. He spurred his horse on, watching the ranch now.

Men were tumbling out of the bunkhouse, running toward the corral. The two women and the boy ran from the main house, following the riders.

They drove for the corral where the foreman was throwing a saddle on a horse and Harden shouted.

'Our guns. Where are our guns?'

Sands' face was blank with astonishment for a second, but he was quick. 'In the bunkhouse.'

'Get them, Luke.' Harden threw himself to the ground. 'Which horses do the women ride?'

Sands pointed at the chestnut. One man had just got a rope on it. Harden yanked a saddle off the fence, not knowing or caring if it was the proper one, and ran toward the mincing, excited animal.

Dust, confusion filled the corral. Harden got the saddle on the chestnut, left it for the other man to secure and ran for another. Ethel raced past him with Tommy and his mother just behind her. Her head swiveled and her eyes widened but she did not stop for questions. Bell caught the boy and heaved him up to a horse he had just saddled. The boy's mother—Harden did not even know her name—caught a rope as a man held it toward her, pulled the horse down and Harden threw a saddle on it, tightened the cinch, lifted her to the stirrup.

Three riders, mounted now, were out of the corral, firing at the onrushing line of Indians. Purdy galloped from the bunkhouse, Harden's gun belt over one shoulder, two rifles waving in his big hands. He tossed one rifle at Dave, dropped to one knee and began firing, slowly, steadily, in a paced rhythm that held no panic.

Harden caught the rifle, set himself and

joined the shooting. One Indian pony collapsed, threw its rider over its head. The dark figure lay twisted, still. Another Apache was knocked down.

A sharp, choking cry near him told Harden that one of the ranch crew was hit. Then Sands was beside him, matching the rhythm of his shots with his and Purdy's.

The range now was barely a hundred yards. The repeating rifles of the crew kept up a constant rattle of sound.

Purdy's spotting the Apaches when he did had spoiled what was intended as a surprise attack. They did not like this pointblank action. Harden saw the racing rank break, split and swing away. He stopped firing at once to save ammunition and called to Sands.

'Hold it. Is there a back way out of here or is this a box canyon?'

The foreman shot again before he spoke, and let go a Confederate yell as a savage spun off his pony and lay sprawled where he fell.

'Got him. They're running. We licked them.'

Harden shouted to catch his attention, then said, 'Don't be a fool, they'll be back. But they'll take their time if we're penned up here. Can we get out behind the buildings?'

Sands blinked, then nodded. 'Yeah. There's a side canyon goes up to the mesa. It's steep and it's narrow. Only room for single file, but it goes through.'

'You take the women and the boy. Get them

out of here before that crowd comes back.' He had no hesitation at giving orders here. He was certain he had more experience with Apaches than any of these men.

He swung around for a fast survey of their forces. Two men were down, one beside the corral fence, one in front of the house. His full sweep brought him back to Sands, still there.

'Damnit, get the women away.'

Sands finally moved, jumped for his horse and Harden called to Purdy.

'Take a look at those two on the ground.'

With those two out of it, with Sands gone, only Bell and Fenner were left. He shouted at them.

'Mount up and follow Sands. Hold the canyon mouth until we get there.'

Neither argued. Both were obviously glad to be away.

Purdy came back saying, 'Those two have had it.'

'Did you break their guns?'

Purdy gave him a hurt look. 'And got what cartridges were left in their belts.'

Across the meadow, well out of range, the Indians were milling around in a council of war.

Harden said, 'Let's go,' and ran for his own horse. He wished he could take the mule, but that would slow them down. He did open the corral gate, praying that the horses would wheel out, that the Apaches would waste precious time running them down. It was the best possible bait for a people known as the greatest cavalry in the world. Then he mounted and drove after Purdy, around the house.

The canyon opened directly behind the bunkhouse, the entrance blocked by a fence and gate to keep cattle from straying. The stream that wound across the bowl came down out of it, a small, rushing torrent. The trail climbed above it on a narrow rock shelf. Like so many he had found in the Sierra it was little more than a knife cut between sheer walls too steep, too high for a man to climb.

Fenner and Bell waited there, uneasy. Harden waved them on.

'Go on up. Get with Sands and the women. Find some place you can hold if the Indians get past me. Go with them, Luke.'

The big ex-sergeant rolled his eyes. 'You going to try to stop them all alone, Dave?'

'I need you up there. Keep your eye on these two. I don't want them shooting me when I ride in.'

The Negro hesitated a moment longer, then motioned Fenner and Bell ahead of him and trailed them out of sight around the first bend.

Behind them Harden rode with his eyes on the rock walls on both sides. In two hundred yards he found what he hoped for, a short waterfall where the constant hammering of the stream had undercut the wall and left a cave that roared with dull sound.

He swung out of the saddle, took the dynamite sack and stepped into the chill water, careful of his footing as the current boiled around his legs. He had to bend until his face was almost in the water to walk into the cave, and there he planted the sticks, pressing them into crevices in the ceiling, pinched in the caps and fastened the coil of fuse. He backed out, unrolling the coil, draping it over a jut of rock and returned to his horse. He led it on up the canyon, around a turn, feeding the coil out along the dry, scrubby growth that he found rooting in the wall.

At the turn there was a place where by standing on his saddle he could climb to a jutting perch that had been long used by birds, but from it he could see down canyon.

Time dragged out far longer than he had expected. He began to think the Apaches had abandoned the chase, had satisfied themselves with the ranch horses. Then there was a moving shadow on the wall of the bunkhouse and a near-naked figure on a horse moved cautiously into sight and stopped, looking up the canyon mouth.

Others joined him and there was another conference. From their gestures he could tell that they were arguing, expecting a trap of some kind. Slowly one advanced, riding carefully into the mouth, watching the walls. He came around the first bend and stopped, his eyes searching the trail above. Then he gave a signal and four other Apaches rode up to him.

Harden waited until they were together at the bend, then he eased down, dropped from the saddle, lit the fuse and threw himself on his horse again. He drove up the trail, counting time. Perhaps he counted too fast. The explosion was overdue. His lips tightened and he pushed the horse harder.

And then it went. Among the echoes that riccocheted between the walls was a raining clatter and bits of shattered rock showered down around him.

Again he left the saddle and climbed to a height where he could look along the trail. The trail was no longer there. The canyon was no longer there. It was wholly blocked, filled two-hundred-feet deep as concussion brought the high wall down. There would never again be a trail this way from the ranch to the mesa top.

There was no sign of the Apaches who had reached the bend, and the ranch buildings were out of sight behind the new, jumbled barricade. He was satisfied with the job. The Indian raiders could not follow them this way. The best they could do would be to circle around by the main trail. That would take time, time that could be used for escape.

He mounted again and rode three miles further up the tortuous grade before he crested out on the flat mountain top. Purdy was the first one he saw as he came over the edge. The others were behind the Negro. They had either not found a hiding place or the blast had brought them out again. They rode toward him in a group, Sands ahead, the women and the boy behind him.

'What the hell happened?' It was Sands.

'I blew the wall down on some of our friends.'

'Blew the wall . . . what with?'

'Had some dynamite in my pack.'

Ethel Mayfield kicked her horse ahead of Sands. Her voice was hoarse with some great apprehension.

'Where did you blow it?'

'At that undercut cave. There's two hundred feet of stone across that place now . . .'

Ethel Mayfield's shriek stopped him. 'The cave . . . The cave . . . My God . . . The treasure was in the back of that cave . . . Our treasure . . .' Her voice died although her lips kept moving.

He stared at her, then shook his head. 'I didn't know. It isn't there now. There's no cave, nothing. It would take a hundred years to dig out that rock slide.'

She spurred at him, raising her crop, beating at him, yanking her horse onto its hind feet, lashing at his head. He saw again the mad flame in her burning eyes, threw up his arm and veered his animal away. He thought for a while that she would drive him back over the edge. Then suddenly she wheeled, rammed in her spurs and drove across the mesa.

That, he knew, was the end of the Tayopa treasure. And unless they all moved fast now it would be the end of them. There were a lot of Apaches who were not caught in his blast.

## CHAPTER TEN

Victorio, chief of the Mimbreño Apaches, was one of the many in this foraging party who had not ridden after the white people. He had sent only a handful of young men in that pursuit and deployed the rest of his force toward his main goal of finding food. But like a good general he must first make sure a white ambush had not been left behind. Dressed in his new fine hat and velvet coat he himself led one group to explore the big log house, and he was inside when the explosion rattled the windows and shook the walls. He hurried out through the back in time to see the cloud of rock dust mushroom above the canyon wall, then rain down with the sound of heavy hail, and he sent scouts up to investigate.

Victorio was a wily and trusted leader with his heart turned to stone against the white man. Trained and tried by the great Mangas Coloradas, he had served under that chief with love until Coloradas was murdered. That murder, after 'Red sleeves' had surrendered, Victorio would never forget nor ever forgive. No Apache in the West would trust any white man again. For years now they had taken vengeance in the burned ranches, the women used, then torn apart, the children's bodies left looking as if they had been worried to death by animals. Prospectors, stage drivers, cowboys died and were left in the hills as mute testimony to the endless variety, the imaginative cruelties of the People in their frustration and fight for survival.

When his braves came running from the outbuildings they were searching, Victorio ordered them to continue and would not let them gather until the scouts returned. Then he called everyone in to listen.

The narrow defile was filled high with a barricade of rubble that could not be scaled, and like the cliffs rising at that end of the valley, the canyon walls were too high, too sheer even for an Apache to climb. The white people were out of reach.

Victorio dismissed them from his mind for the time. He had more urgent business than the triviality of taking a few scalps. Behind him in those bleak mountains that Harden and Purdy had found so barren of life he had left nearly two hundred people in hiding, his old, his women, his children. And they were starving.

The year had not been kind to Victorio,

despite the fact that he had routed his enemies in many encounters. Ever since the murder of Red Sleeves, the People had been under increasing pressure. The American army had herded them onto reservations, lied to them, starved them, decimated them. Victorio had bided his time and counseled his young men to patience. He had even agreed to settle on a reservation, but when he heard that his tribe would be shifted to the San Carlos agency, the one most hated by the Indians, his gorge was filled.

Within twenty-four hours after receiving the order to move Victorio and thirty of his braves vanished from the reservation. The army chased him as far as the border, but Victorio crossed into the safety of Mexico. Word that he was free spread and soon some two hundred Mescalero families joined him. Also, about fifty Bronco Apaches filtered in to his camp. These were outlaws, acknowledging no allegiance to either the American or Mexican authorities and having little respect for their own tribal leaders. Refusing to be settled on reservations these men had taken to the hills, wild as lobo wolves, hunting in twos and threes, but now they came to join Victorio for mutual survival, swelling his band to over a hundred warriors.

The women, the children, the old people hampered him only a little. For three years he had played tag with the whole army of the

Southwest, had raided in western Texas, through New Mexico and the hills of Arizona, striking out of Mexico and recoiling back to it in arrogant defiance.

But this season the tables were turned and everything went wrong. First, Major Morrow with ninety-eight troopers of the Ninth Cavalry had surprised his camp at Ojo Caliente, killed three Indian women and recovered sixty horses and mules that the Apaches had taken from the army. Victorio and most of his people escaped but Morrow hung on his trail, driving him, allowing him no chance to rest until the troops themselves were too exhausted to go on. Freed of that harrassment Victorio had struck back, murdered a dozen ranchers and their families in Texas before he was again driven south of the border.

Usually the Apaches felt safe down there. They established a rancheria in the Candelaria Mountains and raided the neighboring ranches to replenish their horse herd. This year the Mexicans tried to stop them. Don José Rodriguez led a party out of Carrizal looking for them, but rode into one of Victorio's now famous traps. The Mexicans were wiped out and so were fourteen others sent out to avenge them. Those massacres had backfired, roused fury in the Mexican authorities, and a cry for reprisals.

Victorio slipped his band quietly into Texas again, but this time the army was waiting for him and like a cornered coyote he doubled back. Ordinarily he seldom ventured west of the Río de Bavispe, but with the whole eastern slope of the Sierra Madre crawling with Mexican troops he had nowhere else to go, and he was crowded up to a rugged, empty plateau high in the mountains.

It was a good place for defense, and they were not likely to be pursued there. The Mexicans were wary of the area, knowing that aside from the Apaches they were apt to run afoul of the fierce Yaquis living on the western slopes. But there was not enough game in that land to support three hundred people and their bellies were dangerously empty. The band had run out of choices. Victorio left sixty braves to guard the community and took the rest westward in search of food.

By chance they followed the branch trail to Yecroa. They fell upon the pueblo just after daylight and within a quarter of an hour every man, woman and child was dead. Before they killed Don Tomás they questioned him under torture. This pueblo was too poor to fulfill their needs. Where, west of there, could they find more, particularly horses? And Don Tomás had told them about the ranch.

If he had not, Victorio might have been content with the game on the big mountain the trail crossed, but a ranch offered much more than mere meat and they rode on.

The ranch turned out to be a bonanza. The

storeroom yielded barrels of flour, beans, coffee, cured meat, a precious fifty new rifles and plenty of ammunition. The bunkhouse and main building gave up blankets and clothes to a people who delighted in bright and ornate costume, fancy dresses and ornaments to take back to lift the spirits of the women, much to pleasure the men.

As important as the guns was the find of over a hundred horses in the far corral—horses to carry out the wealth of salvage, horses to ride, horses to eat. An Apache would eat anything. The years of near starvation in the desert lands had hardened their lean stomachs to accept a desert mouse, a jack rabbit, a lizard or snake, but the horses were prime food after their other virtues had been used up.

The fat cattle herd in the lush valley did not interest Victorio. A cow was slow to move, hard to drive through that tortured land, the sinew of a range-fed steer tasteless and stringy. A major complaint against the reservations was the beef the government contractors furnished, usually the poorest, scrawniest animals that could be found, that no one else would buy from the supplying ranches. But a horse could be ridden, serve as a pack animal, pull a travois, and finally, when it was eaten, its taste was rich and sweet.

So Victorio came as near smiling as his creased face ever did. He had humor, but it was not a humor the white man understood. With the bounty here assuring his people of food for a while, with the spiritual satisfaction of the massacre at Yecroa behind him, he permitted himself amusement at the warriors here plundering the buildings, playful now, capering, dressing in the white men's and women's finery. From childhood he had been taught to mask his emotions and it would be a loss of face for a war chief to show pleasure as if he were an ordinary man, but his fierce eyes lighted at the sight of Manah coming out of the house.

Manah was a Bronco, square, tall for an Apache, with a thin hawk face and cruel eyes. He had found Colonel Mayfield's Confederate uniform and dress sword. He wore the slouch hat rakishly, the coat with its tails flapping around his bare, brown legs, and the sword belted about his waist. He was fit to laugh at.

Victorio did not really like Manah. He respected him as a good warrior, a shrewd and ruthless killer, but he did not have the quality that Victorio prized above all else, unwavering loyalty to his own kind.

Manah could not he trusted when his own interests were not at stake. Manah was greedy. He spent himself too much on white women. Victorio knew that Manah had turned from a set course more than once, endangering the party, to attack a small ranch only to use the woman there, then kill her. The killing at least was good, but the man's lawless independence and refusal to bow to tribal authority was not good.

Manah came to Victorio, parading, turning himself about to show off the full effect of his elegance.

'Two women were here, one small boy,' he said.

Victorio counted. Blankets on five mattresses in the bunkhouse. Three beds in the house slept in. Two ranch hands dead in the yard, scalped. It added to three men, two women and a boy escaped up the canyon. About Dave Harden and Luke Purdy he knew nothing. He regretted that he did not have time to run them down. If he lived to be a thousand and killed a white every day, Victorio felt that he could never even the score for the murder of Mangas Coloradas. Just now, though, getting food back to the encampment was the first imperative. But as he expected, Manah had his own priority.

'I want those women.'

Victorio told him, 'We have already been gone five days and even if we travel day and night it will be three more before we can reach the people. They will be very, very hungry.'

Manah's thin mouth turned down. He did not dare deny Victorio directly here. Too many of the party were Mimbreños and gave full loyalty to their chief and even the Broncos would not necessarily accept him as their leader. But he could not let this opportunity pass.

'You have warriors enough to take back the food and drive the horses. It will not feed the people quicker if some of us stay a while to hunt,' he argued.

Victorio gave no hint of the relief he felt. The Bronchos were all troublemakers and there had already been friction on this ride. It would be best for all if some of them did separate for the return. But to maintain his command he did not want to appear to give in too easily.

'We will discuss it when we are all together, when we have finished here,' he said, and walked away to close the subject.

They stripped the place of everything they could use or that caught their fancy, made up bundles and loaded the horses. They set the sacked buildings afire and moved down the meadow out of range of the heat, and there Victorio called a council. He stood with the flames eating the shake roof of the main house as a background and spoke. He did not mention the women. That would be impolite.

'The white people have escaped to the top of the mountain,' he began. 'We cannot all give the time to go after them. Our families depend on us to bring them food. But Manah has asked permission to lead a party to take the scalps.' His eyes ranged over the warriors and saw which eyes flamed with desire. 'I cannot tell you what to do, but those who are not of my family I release. None need go. Those who wish to shall acknowledge Manah as their leader.'

No one moved. The time was not quite yet. Victorio was not finished. He gave a little while for them to search themselves and find if they could accept his restriction, then moved aside, away from Manah, and said, 'Whoever chooses Manah, go to him now.'

Ten men went to stand with the Bronco and Victorio raised his hand to them in the sign of fortune, the informal appeal to the gods to bring success to the venture.

Manah showed his pride that such a war chief as Victorio had honored him with this authority. He had no doubt of his ability to track down the whites and deal with them in a manner fitting to the memory of all those Apaches who had fallen. But it was good to know that those who would ride with him must bind themselves to obey his command. He stood solemn as the ten came to him, Gian-na-tah first. He passed his open palm before the man, felt the light touch as the other passed a palm across his own in the sign of fealty that ran back into the shadows of their history. When they had all so sworn, Manah turned back to Victorio and completed the ceremony of allegiance in the same manner.

The old chief then told the younger man, 'Arm your men with our new rifles that shoot many times. You will keep them safe and bring them to the rancheria with the scalps.'

Manah was more than pleased with this largess. Victorio was not only letting him go, he was sending him generously equipped, and Manah understood that in this way Victorio himself would take part in the chase. He lifted the guns out of the case broken open on the ground, handed one with a box of ammunition to each of his party.

When they were distributed he led his men in a great shout, the high, wild, frightening cry that had transfixed settlers all along the frontier for more than twenty years, the cry for blood, for vengeance, for justice. Then the Broncos ran like happy colts for their mounts, shaking the rifles above their heads.

Turning their backs on the leaping flames and rolling smoke the two parties rode out together, past the dike, and took the road to the trail they had come in by, climbing the flank of the big *cerro*, to get to the mesa top.

## CHAPTER ELEVEN

When Ethel Mayfield had bolted hysterically off through the trees, Sands had wheeled his horse and driven after her. Fenner, the big, brutish man who had tried to keep Harden and Purdy out of the ranch when they first found it, was in a near panic, white-faced, sweating, cursing, his little eyes bugging, frozen on the canyon.

'Let's get out of here before them damn devils come up after us.' He was talking to the other ranch man, Bell, his voice a croak.

Bell's lip curled up, pulling at the scar that ran from his cheekbone down to his mouth, giving the effect that the sneer covered half his face.

'You so scared you want to run out on the women? Nobody's coming up here for a long piece, because there's no place to get up. I don't know much about Apaches but I do know they can't fly.'

Bell sat his horse protectively close to the brown-haired girl, one hand stroking her animal's withers as though, not daring to touch her, he wanted to make her feel his presence. He looked speculatively at Harden, who, in spite of the treatment they had given him so far had fought with them and made the escape up here possible.

'What about you and the nigra now? Which way are you going to jump?'

Watching the reactions of the ranch men during the brief fight at the ranch Dave Harden had seen that although all of them had fought in the Confederate army the word Apache had terrified them, rattled them. He tried to weigh the chances. For himself and Purdy alone he knew that given an even break they could get away. But two women and a child could cut the odds and what help the men would be was doubtful.

'We'll stay,' he said. 'Let's find out where we're at. We've got a little time if they have to detour to get at us. I've fought Apaches. They'll spend a while ransacking the place, then they'll burn it. After that they'll look for us. We should be gone from here by then.'

Bell's eyes widened with a new fear. 'They'll find the guns . . . fifty repeating rifles . . . ammunition . . .'

The foreman, Sands, came back leading the Mayfield woman's horse with her astride, rigid and vacant-eyed, and he paid no attention to anyone but her, trying to talk to her, trying to get a response that did not come. He was as useless at this point as Fenner.

Harden said, 'Time to move. We'll cut across the mesa for Yecroa. There are people there who will fight if they're warned.'

In his low, soft voice Purdy said without emphasis, 'Not any more there aren't.'

Harden's head snapped toward him with his silent question.

Purdy nodded down the canyon. 'You didn't see that Indian down there with Don Tomás' hat on . . . and his coat?'

The picture flashed back to Harden. He had not had his sights on that particular Apache; it had not really registered on him until now. A thread of thin, gold stringer running through rocks he would have spotted at once, but Purdy had been quicker than he in this most important observation.

Acknowledging this, he asked the Negro, 'So where do we go?'

Purdy sounded thoughtful. 'That big canyon where Tayopa was . . . plenty to eat off there . . . Did you mean it when you said it was a taboo place to Indians? Does that include Apaches? Even if it don't we could hold it at that narrow gate.'

'If we could get there, yes. But how do we do that when the road in is the one the Apaches are using?'

Purdy's mouth rounded in a silent whistle.

Then Bell spoke, 'There's a way down west of here, a hogback I found when some stock broke through the fence and got up here. About ten miles to it and it drops back to the trail way below the ranch.'

'Let's go.'

They lined out as the first plumes of lazy smoke came above the turn in the canyon that blocked their view below.

Bell took the lead, putting his back to the early sun, twisting through the mesa trees, telling the brown-haired girl, 'Miz Carol, you and Tommy come right behind me and stay close,' and saying sharply to Sands, 'You bring Miss Ethel next, and look alive. Be more help to her if you watch out for Indians.'

Fenner, gray-faced, crowded into line

behind Sands and rode with his rifle across his lap, his head swinging from side to side, expecting Apaches behind every bush and tree trunk. A deer lying hidden in the thick undergrowth bounded up and away when the horses came too close. Fenner whipped his gun toward his shoulder and fired before he could aim, before he knew what he was shooting at. Sands turned in his saddle and cursed him.

'What the hell? Quit that. We're short enough of lead to begin. You want to tell them right where we are?'

Fenner shook himself, blew out his breath and tried to settle down, but he was dangerously spooked. Luke Purdy looked at Harden and in his eyes Harden saw something that had not been there before, a chill pleasure in Fenner's fear. If Fenner was the man Purdy had come to find, the black man was going to enjoy watching the poison eat through him, and he kneed his horse in after him where he could keep close track of Fenner.

Harden brought up the rear where he could see all of them. He called to Bell.

'How long is it going to take the Indians to find a way up here?'

The man was long in answering. 'If they use the Yecroa trail, about two hours. If they know this mountain better than I do . . . maybe sooner. A goat couldn't make it in less than an hour.'

They reached a clearing where the

underlying rock of the mountain surfaced and only stubble grass grew, and as if he felt the pressure of pursuit Bell put his horse to a gallop. Harden called again.

'Easy. Easy. You're going to need that animal.'

Reluctantly Bell slowed, got control of himself, and from there on there was no talking. Harden hung back out of the noises of riding, to listen. Nearby birds cried the warning of their passing but further away there were no sounds of disturbance. With his ears tuned to pick up any sign of riders behind, knowing that not even an Apache can take a horse through country filled with animals without alarming them, he let his mind range over the makeup of the party, to decide what he had best do.

In a showdown Purdy would fight well. Sands and Bell had stood their ground in the skirmish and would probably do so again. Fenner . . . Fenner was a question mark. In his present state he would panic. But if they made it to the valley without being attacked that safe time might strengthen him. If the Apaches caught up with them short of the valley? Dave Harden took three bullets out of his belt and put them in a separate pocket. For the two women and the boy. So that he would not in the heat of a battle forget and use up that last recourse.

Then a sour smile touched his mouth. What

was he doing, playing God? Bell up there in the lead was plainly concerned, first with the girl he called Miz Carol, Colonel Mayfield's widow, and Harden thought there was more than the respectful duty of an employee in his interest. So Bell should be responsible for her and the boy. But Bell said he didn't know much about Apaches, so he had better be forewarned what to expect when they captured a white woman alive.

Next there was Sands, so wrapped up in Ethel Mayfield that he appeared to have forgotten why they were on this ride. He too would have to be told, and pretty bluntly, to get through his preoccupation. He was at her side now, reaching to touch her shoulder, to clamp his hand over hers, folded on the high pommel, talking to her, urging her to answer him.

Ethel was not answering, not even turning her head. She rode rigidly erect and gave no sign that she knew anything that was happening around her or where she was. Harden had seen a miner in shock once. A powder charge had gone off prematurely while the man was tamping the hole. It had not hurt him but he had stood frozen as rocks rained around him. The foreman had called to him, shouted at him, cursed him in three languages, slapped him hard in the face without effect. To Harden it had seemed cruel, inhuman. Then the foreman had swung a pick handle against the miner's head. The man dropped. Harden had jumped for the foreman but had been hauled back by other men of the shift. A few minutes later they had revived the clubbed man and aside from a sore head he was normal. He could not recall even the blast.

Harden wondered if a sudden blow might not jar Ethel back to reality, but he did not dare try. Watching Sands, he knew that if anyone touched the woman the foreman would kill him.

For a while he concentrated on listening for far sounds again, and when there were still none he went back to thinking about Purdy. If they reached the valley and held it against an Apache siege, how long would it be before the black man managed to learn whether Fenner was missing two toes? And if Fenner was Seth Slade, one-time slave catcher, what would Purdy do? Kill him at once when they still needed his gun for whatever it was worth? Drive him outside to the mercies of the Apaches? If he did either, what would he do next? He had no reason to love any white people. Would he consider the women and child as worthy of protection, or as white enemies? Would he stay? Or try to slip off alone?

Dave Harden decided that only Sands and Bell could be relied on in a final extreme. And he had seen at least forty Indians in the ranch attack. Well, at least he had found the lost

111

mines of Tayopa. And he had pretty good evidence that the treasure had existed as the old Mexican way back in the early spring had said it did. He could not take these satisfactions into a next world, if there was one, but he could appreciate them while he lasted in this one.

Bell's trail led fairly straight across the mesa top, giving somewhat around knobs and areas of thick brush. The maximum two hours of grace passed, and another two. Harden called an occasional short rest. The first time the southern men argued, Fenner in particular, urgent to keep going.

'These horses are all we have,' Harden told them. 'If they break down we'll be afoot. We'll be ridden down. Apaches are not stupid. They won't run their animals into the ground, they'll rest theirs too. They may close up on us some, but our best chance is not to push too hard.'

They were cavalrymen, and finally they understood, but they could not relax as Harden did, as Purdy did, conserving energy they would need later. Harden also took that opportunity to lead Bell and Sands aside and convince them of what must be done about the women and the boy in a final eventuality. He had a hard time making them see that too. They looked at him with sick eyes, fighting against believing, until Harden described in vivid detail a burned-out ranch and what remained of the people there that he had

112

come upon in a summer of prospecting in Arizona Apache country.

The rancher had been stripped and tied spread-eagled against his corral fence, riddled with spear holes in nonvital places, dried blood caked in empty eye sockets, although Harden could not say whether that was Indian work or the later feasting of buzzards. His scalp had been taken of course, and the lower flesh of the body roasted, hanging over the cold charcoal of a slow fire. The dirt yard in front of the man was trampled by many moccasined feet, the prints still clear around the naked woman's body. She had been a young woman as well as he could judge by what was left— mass-raped, the legs and arms hacked off, breasts cut away, the face and torso bird-eaten. He had found the animal-torn bodies of three children with skulls crushed in against the cabin wall.

They were southern men before they were soldiers, with a southern chivalry toward women. Bell went further into the bushes and Harden heard him retching. At the sound Sands made a hurried short excursion of his own. When they came back each of them showed Harden three bullets in their hands before they dropped them into their shirt pockets.

'We been down here near seven years,' Sands said. 'I've heard the stories. I didn't believe them.'

113

'Believe them,' Harden said. 'Let's move on.'

The sun climbed high. In the open spaces the day was hot, like a heavy weight on them. The wind seared them. Under the trees there was some relief and the shade cooled the breeze. They had no canteens, could not carry water, but the mesa was cut by creeks and that was not a problem. None of them had eaten since the night before, but they could not risk a shot at any game nor take the time to make and use a snare. Food would have to wait.

They reached the hogback and before they started down they stopped for a fourth rest beside the stream that plunged almost as steeply as a waterfall along its base. Sands lifted Ethel off the horse and sat her on the ground against a rock like a stiff-jointed doll, but this time as he dropped beside her her wide eyes followed him, though still without a change of expression.

Harden saw that and saw too that the little boy was giving out. He lay beside his mother and buried his face in her lap, not crying openly but trying to stifle a whimper. She stroked his blond head, her own bent over him, whispering, encouraging. In the haste of escape from the ranch the pony he had ridden when Harden first saw him had not been caught up, and his own saddle was too small for the big horse he had been given for this ride. The saddle he was using was too big for him, the horse's barrel too wide. He could not reach the stirrups and had ridden with his toes tucked into the loop of the strap from which they hung. Now after a day of bravery he was very tired. When Harden called an end to that rest he went to Carol Mayfield and squatted on his heels beside her, putting his face on a level with hers and smiling.

'You ought to be proud of that boy, Ma'am, he'll grow up to be a fine man. He looks a little tuckered now and there's still some ways to go. Let me take him up with me while we go down this hill.'

Her eyes were shocked. She had not, Harden thought, been expecting to survive. All day she had ridden with drooping, defeated shoulders, and he had spoken of the boy growing up deliberately. Her reaction told him what he wanted to know. The shock passed quickly and she returned the smile, wanly, but she returned it, and said a soft thank you. So there was a fiber of strength there. She might need it.

'Okay, Button,' he said and picked the boy up and carried him to his horse, lifted him to the saddle and swung up behind him, crooked an arm about the small body. 'Just lean back and rest yourself.'

Carol mounted and without a word pulled her horse in at Harden's side. Bell, helping Sands get Ethel in her saddle again, turned from that task, saw the new arrangement and bridled.

Harden said quickly, 'I'll watch out for them. You've got a trail to make, and if it's like the rest of this country it could be tricky.'

For a moment he thought the rider would argue, then the man subsided.

'It is. Mind her good.'

Harden reached for the rein of Tommy's horse and led it back to Purdy, but Purdy smiled his new, close smile.

'Give it to Fenner and you go ahead of him. I'll ride drag but I want him right ahead of me. All the way.'

It annoyed Harden. This was not a time to let your mind dwell on a personal vendetta, and the annoyance showed in his words.

'Keep your ears open for bird chatter behind us. They'll give first warning.'

Purdy's mouth spread then in a wide, mocking grin. 'Teach a dog to suck eggs? My scalp lock may be short but I like it where it is.'

So they turned down the hogback. It was not too steep at the top and wide enough at first that Carol could ride abreast of Harden. She saw her son relax and his lips stop trembling. Soon, lulled by the swaying gait of the walking horse and the security of the man's body gently rocking and his arm around him, Tommy dropped to sleep.

Carol was roused out of the stupefaction that the threat behind had held her in by this stranger's apparent assurance that they could get away from the Indians. She was now acutely aware. With awareness came impatience with the slow pace at which they moved, a snail's pace it seemed to her, and looking back beyond Purdy she saw the hoof marks of the eight horses plain to follow. In a voice too low to wake the boy she spoke to Harden.

'Shouldn't we be hiding our tracks?'

'No use,' he said. 'An Apache can track over bare rock. Waste of time.'

He looked at her, studying how this would hit her, and really saw her for the first time, relieved of the stupor that had made her face a mask. It was a face too thin to be beautiful, framing large, dark eyes haunted with sadness. The chin was firm and the mouth composed in quiet resolution that bordered on resignation to despair.

She did not turn her head to look back again but rode with her eyes forward, unconsciously settling her body as if into some familiar chair, retreating into some posture of old habit. Broken out of the paralysis of terror she could think again. Only so much fear could be absorbed. After that the edge was dulled. She knew. She had lived in fear all of her life, lived in silent desperation under forces too strong for her to overcome. Only for a few dazzling weeks had she ever known hope.

First there had been her father, a sailor come ashore to run a limping, stinking hide and tallow factory on the swampy reaches of the Gulf coast, stern, taciturn, ignorantly cruel and soured by the shadow of failure that never lifted from him. He had worked her mother to death before Carol was ten. Then he worked her, quick to use his belt on her, vicious when he was drunk.

When she was twelve he took a horse in trade, was too lazy to look after it and gave it into her care. It was the only thing she felt was hers. After that she kept out of his way as much as she could, spent hours riding through the flat country, went home when she had to and submitted to the beatings because she was too young and frightened to run away.

When she was fifteen she met Mayfield. She was riding, miles from town, and the horse went lame. She got down and led it, the pain of every limping step hurting her, tears running. The young man came riding, overtaking her. He got down gallantly, a fair-haired giant with a vitality that overwhelmed her. He laughed at her tears and dried them with his handkerchief. He saw a girl browned golden by so much sun, thick, brown braids that had captured copper glints from the sky, brown eyes too big for the face, deep pools of compassion for the horse. He took her up to his saddle with him and felt a young body strong from so much riding, beginning to bloom. He took her into town and saw to the doctoring of the lamed animal.

He was not a colonel then. He was out recruiting, raising the company he meant to lead east to New Orleans and the new Confederate army. He was Tom Mayfield, orphaned master of the Ward plantation, leading citizen of Orange County. Carol knew who he was because her father had bought cattle from him for the Port Arthur factory, but she had never spoken to him before.

Two weeks later they were married, just before he led his company to war. It was a miracle to escape her father and the ugly life of the tallow factory, the butchering, the constant rancid pall that overhung everything. It was dream stuff to be swept up by this lusty dynamo who laughed at her fears and timidity, to be carried in state to the great house built by Tom's Virginia father, to be attended by respectful slaves, to be dressed in fine clothes, given a room all of her own. And to feel his strong hands on her fresh body, caressing, rousing, teaching, unfolding a meaning to life . . .

Then as suddenly as he had appeared he was gone. Fear came back—fear of the distant war that she did not understand, that was unreal and remote from the flat coastland, and fear of her new sister-in-law.

Ethel Mayfield was her brother's twin. She shared his blue-eyed blondness but not his bronzed, glowing skin. Her face and arms were very light, translucent, and when she rode abroad she protected them with veils and long sleeves and gloves. There were differences in their personalities too. Ethel idolized Tom. If he had brought home a bedraggled cat she would have accepted it and made over it the same way she took in the stray waif of a bride—but only to please him. She stood beside Carol on the wide veranda and watched the big, straight figure canter out along the tree-shaded lane on his way to war. When he was out of their sight she moved a step away. Her chin lifted and her thin-walled, up-curving nostrils flared. Her tall, imperious figure looked down on the shorter girl.

'You understand,' she said, 'that the plantation belongs to Tom *and me*. While he is away I will manage it so that it will be just as he left it when he comes back. You had best keep to your embroidery.'

Not understanding this change, Carol laughed uneasily. 'I don't know how to embroider,' she said.

'No . . . you wouldn't.' Ethel shook her head in impatience. 'The Mayfields are one of the first families of Virginia. I can't imagine what possessed him to marry you. Unless he got you pregnant and was too much a gentleman to send you packing. But it's done. I'll have Mammy-Mu teach you, make whatever she can of you.'

From that day on Ethel put off her crinolines, dressed in trousers and rode the plantation like a male overseer, domineering and hard on her slaves. Carol stayed out of her way and dutifully learned the graces of a southern lady from the old woman who had raised the Mayfield twins under the eye of their Virginia parents. When they met for supper in the hall where white linen glowed and silver reflected the little flames of branched candelabra, Ethel looked first at Carol's belly. When no baby swelled there she was perversely provoked, as though Carol had stolen her way into the family under a false pretense.

Toward the end of the War the Union forces swept through. The plantation was raided. Ethel was caught and misused but Mammy-Mu spirited Carol off into the slave quarters and hid her until the soldiers had ransacked the house and gone. They went through like locusts, took the horses, stripped the storehouses, stole jewelry and whatever of value they could carry. Afterward Carol and Mammy-Mu found Ethel alive in the tumbled bedroom and nursed her back to strength. It did not bring the two white women closer together except that Ethel acknowledged Carol as within a tight core of southerners against everyone else. And Ethel's arrogance, her imperialism froze into a cold, hard hatred and determination to survive.

When Tom rode home a colonel the slaves were freed and gone. Only Mammy-Mu stayed, and the three women were living in a deeper poverty than even that Carol had grown up with. He too was brutally changed. There was no more laughter. There was bitterness, moodiness, sullenness and a determination to match Ethel's. His reunion with his wife, his lovemaking, were no longer gay but subordinated, second to a hard, new dream.

He had found a place in Mexico that they could take over. He had a handful of his company left who would follow him. There were a million cattle running wild through the brakes, rangy offspring of the herds that had wandered off through the war years when there were no men to keep them together. They would gather as many as they could drive and trail them down into the Sierra Madre and begin a new plantation out of reach of the damned yankees.

Carol had never been further than half-a-day's horseback ride from Beaumont. Both Mayfields terrified her now and the new venture sounded like a nightmare. The trip was all of that. In leaving Mammy-Mu behind she left the last kindness she had ever known. They drove ten thousand balky, vicious, mean-eyed cattle through a devastated land overrun by Union soldiers and carpetbagging thieves. A thousand miles.

On the way a howling pack of Indians stampeded a part of the herd. Ethel rode out with the men, to kill with them, to round up the animals with them, a woman of ice. Carol had her baby that day, alone, on the bank of a creek. The baby lived. And she had something to live for.

The child made a difference in the colonel. He had an heir to carry on the Mayfield name. In gratitude he told her the secret behind this monumental flight. It was not only a plantation they were going to establish but a new, independent country. They would start a ranch in a valley he knew that could be defended, and they would look for the treasure of the Tayopa mines. When they found it they would have the money to bring in more southerners and settle a new nation with the degenerate natives for slaves.

Carol had not believed him. She had felt the wind of madness in the twins' fierce drive. But she was trapped. They had reached the valley. They had built the ranch and it had prospered. It had taken six years to find the Tayopa silver. Carol felt hope again. It had been lonely, with the only other woman there despising her, but the colonel had sent most of his crew north to carefully choose and bring down families, and there would be people. Then the snakebite had killed him.

She had drawn apart, helpless while Ethel took command again, obsessed by the new dream country and reaching for Carol's son, trying to take him out of his mother's control.

And a new alliance was formed. The foreman Sands had an underlying brutality that reminded Carol of her father. He was ignorant, without grace, no man that the aristocratic Ethel would be expected to accept as anything more than an employee. But Carol watched her use him arrogantly, then, when he had submitted and she needed his strong hand on the ranch, take him to her bed. Carol did not know, beyond lust, how much of Sands' interest was in the woman, how much in the ranch and silver she controlled. She did know that neither of them considered her a factor. She was all but at their mercy.

Slowly, surreptitiously, since the colonel's death the man Bell had been making his presence known. He had been the colonel's sergeant during the war, loyal and dependable. Since the colonel's death he had done small kindnesses for her and the boy, though not in the colonel's memory. Bell knew she was a woman. She found him gradually working toward the time when she might choose to end her widowhood. As with Sands she thought Bell's appetite was whetted by the ranch, but Bell would stand up to Sands and he was not cowed by Ethel. Ugly as he was with the knife scar disfiguring his face, she had thought the time might come when she would have to turn to him for protection.

Now everything Ethel and Sands and Bell had wanted was gone, the treasure blasted out of existence, the ranch destroyed, and all of them were running for their lives. For herself, she was at the end of the road, ready to finish her life and sink down into the earth where she was.

But there was her son. She wanted the boy to live, wanted him to grow up as the stranger Harden, holding him now, had hinted might be. She put the luxury of giving up away and, as she had taught herself to do through the years, washed out of her mind all thoughts of what could lie ahead.

At the front of the column Bell called back a low warning. The trail pitched down in sharp, steep switchbacks, narrowed to a shelf. Harden pulled up and nodded for her to ride ahead of him, and single file they came out of the trees into the long descent against the open, barren hillside where there was no cover to hide them from pursuit.

## CHAPTER TWELVE

Manah the Bronco was pleased to be free of Victorio and his restraints. On top of the mesa where the trail leveled and angled across toward the valley where the pueblo Yecroa had been, the combined band stopped. Manah pushed ahead of them a way, scouting the ground to learn if the fugitives had come from the canyon to cut this trail, but the only tracks he found were of the Indians' own unshod ponies heading toward the ranch. So his quarry must be still on the mountain. He rode back satisfied.

His band cut a remuda of eleven horses out of the herd, strung them together for easier driving. He lifted his hand to Victorio and watched the old chief take his train out on the Yecroa trail. Then the Bronco split off up through the timber. His purpose was to climb to the highest point, to find a vantage place where he could look down on whatever moved below. The old Apache adage was in his mind. Never let an enemy get above you, never let an enemy get closer to the sky than you.

He did not know this country, but it did not matter. His party was in much better condition than were the whites. They had taken off the looted clothes, made them into bundles and given them into Victorio's care until they got back to the rancheria. The day would be hot and no warrior in his right mind went into a fight hindered by clothing. They carried the fine new rifles. The new horses were fresh, a little fat perhaps for hard riding, but that would soon come off.

True, they were shod, which he did not approve of, and were trained to be mounted from the left side, a slight disadvantage. An Indian mounted from the right and in a skirmish one was apt to forget. When speed was needed a shying horse could mean death. Then, too, these animals were uneasy at the difference between the smell of white riders and Indians, although that would be overcome in a few days, by the time they got back to the encampment.

Manah had no worries. The loneliness of the country that had bothered Harden and Purdy did not affect him. He was self-sufficient. He could survive where a white man could not. There was game here, and mesquite bean, prickly pear, mescal. There was water aplenty on the mountain. Manah had lived for long stretches in the most arid deserts. A pebble held beneath his tongue to make the saliva flow would keep him alive for three days. For longer periods a horse could be killed, gutted, the intestine cleaned and filled with water and transported, wrapped around the horse you rode.

Neither was the Indian in a hurry. Wherever the white people were they would be slowed by the two women and the child, and they had no extra horses to which they could change off. They would have to stop to rest the animals they rode. Manah would have to stop too, but for shorter periods of time. He would catch up to them soon enough, probably this very day that was still young.

They found their high place at a bare rock outcropping and with Gian-na-tah at his side Manah studied the country below him. He could see down over the trees to where they stopped abruptly at the cliffs along whose base ran the trail that passed the mouth of the ranch valley. That sharp cleavage of the land ran west as far as he could see, suggesting that there was no way to get off this side of the mesa for many miles. He saw how far the sun had risen and judged that if the fugitives had gone from their canyon top straight across the mountain toward its north side they would have passed the crest by now. By following along that crest he would cut their tracks. So he made his signal and put his troop at a good clip along the high ground toward the west.

He chose Gian-na-tah as his second in command not out of fondness; the young warrior still had too much playfulness in his spirit to endear him to the hate-forged Manah even if no trace of it showed in the hawk-sharp features. It was the reputation that had earned him his name—Gian-na-tah, Always Ready— on which he counted. Gian-na-tah had proved over and over that he was always ready . . . for anything.

With the map of the land he had looked over in his mind, long experience to tell him how fast he was moving and the hot Mexican sun to keep time for him, he crossed the area where the whites must have passed if they were traveling north. The troop searched carefully and found no sign left by six horses. So they must have headed west.

That decided he turned downhill to come to the cliffs at the upper end of the ranch canyon. There he dismounted his people and sent them scattering in a half circle to pick up exactly the white trail. Manah himself rode down the canyon to the place of the explosion, to make certain his prey had not been able to work down over the dam of broken rock and again reach the ranch valley. One look told him such a descent was impossible and, with all avenues of escape now investigated and only the westward one open, he climbed back to the top ready to move directly.

Gian-na-tah had a surprise for him. He took Manah proudly to show what he had found. The route of the white riders was very clear. No attempt had been made to disguise it, which meant one of two things. Either they were in such a panic that they had not spared the time to try to hide their way . . . or someone was with them who appreciated that they could not be hidden from an Apache. That did not matter. What mattered was Gian-na-tah's horse count. One by one he pointed to the hoof prints, sorting each animal out. There were not only the six that the evidence at the ranch had indicated. There were eight horses in the party, and all of them being ridden. Hopefully, Manah thought, the extra two were other women. That would be a bonus indeed.

And so they rode. It had now been near three hours since the raid. The fugitives could be at most three hours ahead, with the morning still young. Within an hour of following them Manah made another discovery. He had half expected the flight to shake off panic and curve back, up the mesa and around to return to the Yecroa road. He was not concerned about that. Victorio was on that path, moving slowly with the horse herd to control and the burden of so much food and goods. Victorio would, of course, watch his back trail and pick up the whites if they came up behind him.

The prey did not turn back, but neither did it hug the edge of the cliffs hunting a break by which they could get down. Where there was a bulge in the cliff the trail cut straight across, ignoring it, keeping to a definite course through the trees. The whites knew exactly where they were headed.

Before noon the tracks were far back from the cliffs, going toward where the western end of the mesa must be. It appeared to Manah that the people ahead knew of some particular spot that would lead them off the mountain.

Through the afternoon this conviction increased. Further, his quarry was not running headlong. He had hoped they would make a race for safety and run their horses into the ground, but they were not doing so. One after another he found the places where they had rested, dismounted, watered the animals. So the chase would take a little longer. It was a small annoyance. He had no doubt that it would end in women and scalps. All his experience assured him.

The cavalry units sent against his people could seldom travel more than twenty-five miles a day while his own warriors had been known to cover seventy blistering miles of desert hills between sunup and sundown. There were two good reasons for the disparity. The cavalry were weighed down by heavy uniforms, arms, ammunition, gear and trappings not only for ceremonies, while the Apache rode light, bareback, carrying a rifle, a knife and a little bag of shells. Also, the Indian was a far better natural horseman and could get much more out of an animal before it collapsed.

Wherever the white party had paused Manah also stopped and directed his warriors to change from the horses they were riding to those that had been led, which had had no weight to carry for the last miles. They watered the animals but did not stay longer than that took. The men themselves felt no need of rest. Aside from being accustomed to long, uninterrupted rides, their whetted appetites for killing added to their endurance.

Manah felt that he must be gaining on the whites but he had no proof of that until the sun was half down in the western sky. It was then he reached the hogback and the cascading stream. This was the place where the people ahead made a turn out of their daylong course. Nothing about the immediate area suggested that the way down was by the hogback; there had been many hummocks much like it along the trail, but it must be so. The whites had made a considerable rest there.

The Indians again changed horses, and while he was dismounted Manah scouted the ground. Along the edge of the stream he found bootprints. One set the size of a child's foot, another larger but narrower and shorter and daintier than a man's. Manah's black eyes brightened and hung on that print hungrily. The soil was wet but the prints were not yet filled with water. So they were closing in. The three-hour gap was cut perhaps in half, perhaps more. Manah felt an urgency to hurry then, and it became stronger when he found a long, blonde hair caught against a rock. One of the women was yellow-headed, and that was very good. Manah had his own streak of maverick humor, his own second collection of hair besides the scalps such as all of them took. After he used a woman to death he cut a souvenir from her pubic tuft, and he valued these most when the color was golden.

They turned along the hogback through the dense trees and rode another half mile at a faster pace. Quite suddenly they came out of the woods into low brush and bare rock. The ground narrowed to a nose and pitched down on three sides, steep. The hoofprints led along the spine that twisted like a moving snake. Manah stopped his troop to survey the wide expanse laid out below.

From where be sat with Gian-na-tah he could look into the bottom of a shallow canyon, a hundred or so feet deep, running generally east and west. There was a road on the floor, cut deep in the rock by the sharp hoofs of thousands of animals, and reason said that this was the western continuation of the road that passed the burned ranch. From here it wiggled west and was lost in a jumble of rock ridges like a field of snaggled teeth spreading away from the base of the mesa. He could see no movement anywhere on the road.

He could not see the full length down the dropping hogback. In many places the spine curved out of sight behind the higher ground, and there were wrinkles in the sides cut by water running off, deep enough to hide anyone who might be lying in wait there.

The day was dying. Manah's desires cried out to him to make a dash down to the road and along it to fall on his prey before night. But he was alive that moment because he had learned suspicion and caution. The people he hunted could be waiting in any of those hidden spots. Had the positions been reversed, were he being hunted, he would have laid an ambush between where he was and the canyon floor, somewhere along that narrow spine where there was no escape on either side.

'We will scout to the bottom,' he said. 'One man on foot will go down and we will cover him.'

Always Ready was already dismounting when Manah stopped him. 'Not you. You have value to me and there is risk.'

He looked behind him, chose a man from the rank about whom he knew little, and sent him ahead as bait. The others followed well behind but keeping him in sight, their rifles ready in case the scout drew fire. The man moved well. The hogback had not been used enough as a trail that the trace was defined in the rocks. The ground rose and fell, the little hoof scars on stones led around upthrust boulders and sparse growth that had found a tenuous roothold. Looking awkward, the scout was well on balance, ready to throw himself in any direction at the hint of attack. He flitted rather than walked, a copper shadow darting from cover to cover. Even to the fierce, sharp eyes above he was hard to follow. They moved from lookout place to lookout, lower and lower, but no guns exploded. They were still high above him when he reached the canyon floor and turned into the road. There it ran through a narrow defile and they lost him. He was gone what seemed like a long while, then he came out of the mouth of the defile and waved them down.

The sun had sunk below the mountainous

horizon and night came swiftly in this country. They still had light at the top but by the time they had ridden down to the canyon the bottom was in deep gloom. Manah could no longer see the tracks of the horses ahead, but his scout had turned west into the defile, so that was the way they went. In the fading light the defile was a black slot that could hide many dangers. He ordered a camp made where they were.

Danger from the white party was only secondary in his mind. The Apache superstition against fighting at night went back to the beginnings of the People. The dark belonged to the spirits of the dead. In Manah's lifetime that belief had been refortified by Nan-tia-tish. The fiery medicine man had come upon them from the White Mountains, teaching that his ghost dances would call back all the dead Apache warriors who would gather in hordes to fight and drive the white men out of their lands. And according to Nan-tia-tish these warriors who rode at night must not be seen by any living Indian. Whoever did see them would be captured and pressed into their own battle ranks.

Manah was not wholly convinced by Nan-tia-tish. He had not heard of any slaughter of whites that could not be accounted for by earthly men, and when he broke away from his family and took to the wilderness as a Bronco he put away superstition as well as tribal authority.

But a smart warrior must be doubly careful when he took the lonely trail, and why should a sensible man risk angering the spirits, risk calling down their wrath on himself?

So he was taken aback when his lieutenant Gian-na-tah challenged his order to camp and wanted to push on, arguing that the party they hunted would probably stop for the night and this was a chance to come up with them very quickly.

Manah answered, giving all of his reasons, but his ten followers jeered at him. They themselves had used the cover of darkness in Arizona and New Mexico to creep up on isolated ranches, run off stock, resupply themselves with horses, cut the picket lines of the whites who were sent against them. And none of them had ever seen a White Warrior.

They had sworn their fealty to him but they were still Broncos, independent, reserving their ultimate loyalty to themselves. If more than half of them had chosen to accept Manah's decision the rest would have stayed. But all of them were younger than Manah, less steeped in the old teachings, and everyone voted with Gian-na-tah.

Cautiously they entered the black defile, rode through it without mishap and came out into the area of bare, jagged hills cut with deep, dry arroyos. They had starlight to see by then, and they made good time, climbing and dropping. In the arroyo bottoms the night was black. They let the horses choose the way and tuned their nostrils to the smells, hoping for the acrid bite of smoke to tell them the camp was near, and from the tops of the ridges they looked ahead for the red eye of a fire. A suspicion began to grow in Manah that the White Warriors had already found the people he wanted, that men and women and horses had vanished into Nan-tia-tish's limbo. But he said nothing and rode with a quickening pulse. He could not help that and he did not like it. It took the fine edge off his listening ear.

Luke Purdy knew they were there. He could not say exactly what it was he heard, whether it was anything. Perhaps it was only a sense. But there was a change in the night sounds.

He dropped back a quarter of a mile, the better to catch those sounds. He judged without knowing how he judged that Bell and the rest were within two or at most three miles of the main rim of the Tayopa canyon, where the trail turned down along the narrow shelf that dropped in stages to the valley floor nearly a mile below. He wondered if there would be time to reach even the rim. The Apache were getting close. It was like a message whispered through the night.

He was glad at least of the decision taken at the short rest just before dark. Bell had protested that Carol and her son were near exhaustion. He wanted to turn aside, make a camp that might be defended, banking on the Indians stopping where night caught them. Harden had wavered, remembering the dangers of the shelf trail even in daylight, in most places too narrow for two horses to go abreast and with very few spots where an animal could be turned.

It was Carol who had made the decision. In a voice faint with tiredness she had said,

'If the Indians do come there are too many of them to fight. I know the trail, but if Tommy has any chance to live it's in going on.'

Purdy knew now how right she was. He quickened his horse to catch up with them and alert Harden, Sands, Bell who shook up the pace of the tiring horses. Whatever was left in them must be used now.

Purdy stayed close for this drive and they hit the rim earlier than he had expected. There was a moon coming, as yet seen only as a dimming of the stars low on the eastern horizon, and it would be little help when they dropped down the steep wall. Harden spoke to pull the party's mind off the Apaches, draw their full attention to riding, reminding them to let the horses have a loose rein since the animals could see better in the dark then they and instinct would keep them as far as possible away from the drop-off edge.

Bell's horse and finally his hat disappeared as he started down. Sands made a change, getting off his horse, leading it and walking at

Ethel's side with a hand on her knee even though a misplaced hoof might bump him off into emptiness. Carol went next and then Harden, still carrying the boy, who was now awake. Tommy was the only one who appeared to take this descent in stride, with a child's faith in the animal and the man who held him. He had had no experience with Indians and this ride had turned into an adventure.

Purdy watched Fenner go, with Tommy's horse behind him, and sat a while where he was. He heard the creak of saddle leather, the occasional clink as an iron horseshoe struck stone, and then as the trail dropped and turned those sounds were gone. Behind him, faint as the night wind, were very distant noises, but closer there were not the things that should be: the night throbbings that should have risen shortly after he had passed, the call of night birds, the usual scurry of small creatures over the rocks. His hand tightened on the rifle he had carried across his lap ever since dark closed down.

He knew that it could be only his imagination, the anticipation of danger. He had stood night guard in the desert enough to know the tricks the mind played on the ear when you did not want to hear what you listened for.

But then the updraft of the canyon subsided for a moment as a gust off the top pushed it back, and the gust brought a shadow of an odor, and that was not imagination. They were there, moving quietly nearer.

He put his horse down the trail. Three hundred feet below the rim he reached a rock shoulder that the ledge swung around. Everywhere else there was the black void. It gave him a sense of being wholly cut off from reality.

On the far side of the shoulder he looked up, judging the pitch of the sharply slanting rock in the growing moon glow. With luck a man might climb it.

Luke Purdy had learned long before never to hesitate once his instinct had made a decision. He reined the nervous horse to a halt and stepped down gingerly, found footing and felt his way with his boot until he was behind the animal. He clucked to it in a soft sound and slapped the flank lightly with his hand. He did not want to startle it into sudden, dangerous movement. It went away from him and in the darkness he lost sight of it almost at once as it turned the next curve on the descending ledge. Then he was alone, his last contact with a living thing gone with the fading of the slow, chipping steps as the animal felt its way uncertainly down the trail.

He did not wait for total silence. He leaned against the rock shoulder, feeling over it, and found a fissure where the shoulder rejoined the main wall, and explored for pits deep enough to hold the square toes of his boots. He climbed carefully.

The jutting rock was not high. It stopped in jagged, blunt spires about ten feet above the shelf. Twice he slipped, the second time dropping back to the trail with a rattle of small stones. He waited, holding his breath, listening.

No sound came from above. Either the Indians had heard the rattle and stopped or they were not there yet. He took a deep breath and tried the fissure again, his rifle slung over his shoulder, clawing for purchase with both hands and feet, wedging his body into the sharp angle, sliding up the slant.

This time he got a hand over the broken top, tested it for solidity, then dragged himself higher. He eased one leg over the crown of the rock chimney and found a perch like a saddle, with his back against the main wall. There he sat, slipping his rifle free of his shoulder, bringing it around to cover the uphill trail.

He waited a long time. Seconds dragged into minutes, minutes into a quarter of an hour, then an hour. The moonlight increased overhead but did not come into the canyon. The trail below him was barely visible, but Purdy, close against the rock, was in deep shadow. He did not think he could be seen even by an Apache. But the time was coming soon when he could be discovered.

He did not know that the Indians had

141

hauled up back behind the rim for a conference. The strong smell of water came out of the canyon. A fair-sized river, not a slender stream was down there, and it would have to be a fork of the Yaqui. One of the Broncos had heard and now repeated the old story of the massacre of the slave Indians whom the padres had left when they went away and of their ghosts that rose to avenge themselves on later intruders.

'It is a place of the dead,' he said, 'and should be avoided.'

Earlier he had joined in overriding Manah, voted to ride the night. Manah listened deliciously as others turned timorous at this late time, with the droppings of the whites' horses still warm in their nostrils, and found here the chance to reassert his leadership. If there were only slave ghosts, he was not afraid of them.

'I will go alone then,' be sneered, 'if our braves are no longer brave.' And it pleased him to have them wrestle with themselves and not dare to admit before each other that one had less heart than the next. It pleased him also to send the one who had thrown this stone of fear among them as one of two to scout ahead, and to see how cautiously each went over the rim.

Purdy had almost decided that he had been mistaken. He was on the verge of sliding down from his perch and going after the white party on foot. Then a spark of light glinted up the trail from him and there was movement. Hurriedly he laid his arm along the barrel of his rifle, covering it. In his concentration he had not noticed that the glow from the east had grown as the moon rose, but the wink he had seen was moonlight shafting off metal.

In the lessened gloom he saw the figure of a mounted Indian as the Apache brought his horse around the upper curve and stopped, ears, eyes and nose trying to probe the dark ahead of him. He sat motionless, indistinct, with no detail of his head, shoulders, body to be clearly seen.

Purdy did not move. It was an easy shot, not more than two hundred feet. But he did not hurry. He did not want one. He wanted two, three if possible.

The rider came on, moving his horse only a few feet at a time, stopping, moving again. He was within a hundred feet of Purdy before the second Indian materialized around the bend and edged down, paced by the first man as if they were tied together with a rigid bar.

Purdy waited. He must not let the first man pass below him but he wanted to be very sure of getting both. Then the second man called, querulous. Purdy spoke a smattering of Apache but the words were too muted to make out. Then they came again, in starts and stops, hugging the wall. The first rider reached a spot fifty feet uphill from Purdy, the second a hundred feet beyond and stopped there. Purdy could wait no longer. In the next few steps the first man would be sheltered by the slope of the rising wall. He lifted his rifle, took quick aim in case the moon glint betrayed him and squeezed away his shot.

The bullet tore the Apache off the horse, hammered him over the edge. The horse reared in sudden fright. Its forehoofs came down on air and it plunged screaming out of sight. The second rider fired at the gun flash, but too hastily. The lead slapped into the rock below Purdy's foot as Purdy's second shot killed the Indian. He too fell into the chasm but the stunned horse did not move. Purdy shot it deliberately. It crumpled forward on its knees, went to its side and died, miraculously staying on the shelf and blocking the trail.

Purdy knew enough of Apaches to tell him he would not get a shot at a third rider from this position. He swung his leg back over the rocky saddle and dropped to the trail, going downward quickly with one hand against the wall to guide him.

## CHAPTER THIRTEEN

Riding behind Carol Mayfield, Harden heard the shots far back and above him. He twisted in his saddle and peered through the dark, made out Fenner and the boy's horse but could find no sign that Purdy was at the rear. He did not know when Purdy had separated from them but he understood in that instant that the black man had elected to hold the trail alone, to give this warning.

They were in a narrow throat with the canyon wall on one side and a rock upthrust rising from the rim side higher than the head of a mounted man. He could not turn. He could only keep going with the line until he found a wider place.

They all heard the explosions but Bell held the same slow, tenuous pace, as afraid of going off the edge as he was of the Indians. Impatience crowded Harden but there was no way be could move faster, blocked both ahead and behind. The cry of the falling horse came high to begin with, then faded to faintness, and to nothing with the great distance of the drop. The meaning of it slowed Bell even further.

There had been four shots. Had Purdy fired all of them? Or had some of them been Apache guns? Had they killed the one-time sergeant? If they had, then they would now be pressing down on the fugitive train.

The descent seemed interminable until they were out of the slot and there was room enough to dismount, though not to turn a horse around. Harden called softly ahead to Carol, telling her to wait and, with the boy clinging to him, got down on the inside, the horse between him and the edge. He walked forward and passed Tommy up to his mother and, as he lifted him, a sound of a shower of rocks rattling off the trail somewhere above curdled him.

'Go on,' he said in a low voice. 'Ride on.'

She caught the boy against her, sucking in her breath, and womanlike, maternal, said the unnecessary, 'Take care.'

Even in the tension of the moment he had to smile, and silently he thanked her, for the smile relaxed him, made him aware of how taut he was, made him shake himself loose. When you had Apaches to contend with you had to be flexible for quick reaction.

He edged back to let his horse pass him, nudged on by Fenner's animal, snagged the rifle out of the boot and waited while Fenner went by and then the horse the man led. Then be hurried back up the grade.

He was panting by the time a sound stopped him. A horse was coming down. He was on an in-curving stretch with nowhere to get out of sight. All he could do was crowd against the rough wall and set himself, level his gun on the bend around which the animal would come. He saw it emerge, a dark form against the lightening pit of the canyon, and almost fired before he realized there was no rider. He did not lower his gun nor shift the aim, but watched the curve to see if an Indian was there on foot, sending the animal before him as a

146

decoy.

The horse approached, stepping tentatively with no one on its back, no guiding hand on the rein, and stopped in front of Harden, stretching its nose to touch him, blowing, as though the man being there gave it comfort. Harden felt over it and his hand found the shape of Purdy's military saddle.

A blaze of anger burned through him. Purdy was dead. That was his first reaction, that the big man had been shot out of his seat.

Purdy, on his own, had hung back alone, to intercept the Apaches, to try to protect them all, the white people he certainly had no reason to love. Purdy had come to these hills for his own personal vengeance and he had died trying to help those of whom one might be the very man he wanted to destroy.

He pushed past the animal and went on, ignoring caution, but he had not reached the bend before he shook the anger off, crowded it down. He could not go blundering ahead, get himself stupidly killed. Not only his life but the child's, the women's would be horribly forfeited. He must be very, very careful.

He climbed on, setting his feet only when he was sure he would make no noise, disturb no stone. Belatedly he hoped the men below him were not so hypnotized by fear that they would rush on into the big valley without leaving a guard at the gateway, the only place the Indians could be kept out of it. If he was going to give up his life for theirs he did not want it wasted.

As he went higher he was not made more comfortable by the sharp division in the color of the air. The black lower half was cut on a distinctly defined angle from the much lighter upper region as the moon rose over the rim. He could make out shapes of the slanting rock above him now, and soon he would be exposed to the shelf without cover of dark.

And he had not yet found Purdy's body. It might have fallen or been thrown over the edge. He might already have passed the place where he was killed. His hair prickled at its roots at the thought that the Apaches could have come down afoot, scrambled up to hang against the wall over his head and let him go by them into a net. Then it came to him that he had caught no Indian smell and he made himself relax again.

He thought he must be two-thirds of the way up the trail. Around the next bend he would come into moonlight, his movements easy to pick out against the eternal stillness of the wall. Where were they? He stopped where he was, his rifle held easily in both hands, ready to lift on the bend, ready for the first spidery figure that would sift around it and be silhouetted black against the silvering canyon void.

It was not long in appearing. One second there was nothing, the next there was the dark moving shape. He raised the gun. He almost fired, then eased his finger on the trigger. The curve of the shelf between him and the bend was dark, but the half-clip in his rifle gave him six shots, and if more than one Indian came around before the first was too close he might take several.

And then his breath whistled in. The shape had already disappeared into the near gloom but into his mind snapped the after picture of Luke Purdy's campaign hat in his sights. He dropped the nose of the gun and felt his hands shake. On the heels of the thought that he had almost killed the man came another thought. His knowledge of Apaches told him that it was very possible the hat was not worn by Purdy but by the Indian who had shot him.

And so he stood, holding his breath, still watching the bend, straining to hear the footfalls coming toward him. He heard a scuff. It was not a moccasin. A hard boot had made it. Now he called softly.

'Purdy?'

A grunt of surprise came back. At the tightness in the voice that called his name Purdy came on quickly, saying, 'Dave . . . what's wrong?'

Harden was not a particularly emotional man and although he had known many people in his years of wandering he had had few friends, but now his voice trembled.

'I damn near shot you. Thought you were an

Indian. I thought they'd killed you.'

Purdy's low chuckle was dry. 'Not yet. What are you doing up here?'

Harden's whisper was still not quite steady. 'We heard shooting. I figured you were in trouble. Then your horse went by and I knew you were dead. What happened?'

When Purdy had told him Harden asked, 'You don't know how many more there are?'

Purdy shook his head, then realized that Dave could barely see him in the dark and said, 'No. Those two were scouts. They were coming slow and they weren't happy.'

'Let's get out of here.'

'No hurry,' Purdy said. 'They may come as far as the horse on the trail but I don't think they'll want to pass that until daylight. I doubt they'll even try that much tonight, or I'd have stayed where I was.'

Confident as he sounded, Harden noticed that the big man moved downhill just as quickly as he did.

They found Purdy's horse where its rein had caught on a jutting rock and the pressure on the bit had stopped it.

'You ride,' Purdy said. 'You've walked up and down this tightrope enough and I've been resting.'

Harden did not argue. He lifted himself to the saddle and followed as the one-time sergeant felt his way through the dark that was still dense in the lower reaches.

They did not find another mount. Someone in the party might have thought to drop off the horse Fenner was leading, but it had not been done. Harden thought they either believed neither Purdy nor he would come back, or that they were more concerned with having an extra animal for their own relief when they hit the valley. Purdy put it differently when he stopped behind the final bend above the rock slide.

'Don't appear to me that those southern gentlemen put very much store by us, Dave. Now let's see if they had the gumption to guard that cut. And if they did, let's find out if we're going to be let in.'

He raised his voice to haloo ahead. 'Purdy and Harden here. And no Indians.'

He waited in the shelter of the bend for an answer. That the ranch people might exclude them from the valley, keep them outside to face the Apache with no shelter at all, had not occurred to Harden. It told him more than he had ever guessed about what treatment a black man could expect from a white. Purdy took it for granted that even though their guns might be much needed against the Indian force, his color and Harden's unknowing obliteration of their treasure could cause both of them to be denied the safety of the valley. Purdy even smiled bleakly when the high, shrill cry came back.

'Keep away from here. Damn you, you've

151

done enough to us.'

It was the blonde woman's voice. Purdy said, without expression in his tone, 'Well, I guess she got out of her shock all right. What do you suggest we do next, Dave?'

In the moonlight their position was now clear to see. The high wall they had come down continued as one side of the valley in a palisade that could not be scaled. The drop to the valley floor from the ledge was still over two hundred feet and they were blocked ahead by the great rock slide and the guns defending it. Dave Harden looked at Purdy, musing.

'I think I just ran out of suggestions, Luke. Unless we go up the hill again. Maybe . . . '

He was interrupted by another voice from the cut, a man's voice rough with irritation. It sounded like Bell.

'Harden . . . Purdy . . . come on in. She's just hysterical.'

Purdy kicked at a stone with his toe, moving it absently from place to place. He drew a slow breath.

'Well . . . could be all right. One way to find out. I don't much favor going up with only one horse and there ain't much point in just standing here. We get in range, we'll know, and in this light they could miss.'

He stepped out, walking steadily, a bold figure presenting a broad front. Harden crowded close upon him so that the dark bulk of the horse blended with the man's mass and made him a less easy target. They moved into the range of the rifles at the cut. They moved closer. Purdy kept an even, unhesitating pace. They were both well inside reach of the guns now, where if they were fired on a miss would be improbable. And Ethel shrieked again.

'Kill them. Sands, obey me. Shoot them. Shoot them.'

Purdy stopped in mid-stride, stood with his foot lifted, and Harden hauled up the horse to keep from overrunning him. There was no chance to go back. Then they heard Sands curse, heard stones rattle down as if there was a scuffle, and after a time longer than eternity Bell called again.

'Come on. Come on. Sands is taking her back a ways.'

They could still hear the woman crying at Sands, commanding him, then pleading, but the voice was more distant. Purdy put his foot down, completing his broken step, and went on.

Then they were in the cut, and through it, and Bell slid down from the top of the rubble. The people were on the slope, dismounted. Sands held Ethel tightly in his arms while she moaned against his chest. Tommy pressed into his mother's legs, Carol's hands over his shoulders. Fenner stood beside his horse as if on the verge of mounting.

Bell said roughly to Harden, 'Where you been all this time? Where'd you go?'

Harden kept his temper down. The situation was bad enough without adding antagonisms to it. 'You heard the shooting. Luke stayed back to cover you, give you time. He could have been in trouble.'

The southerner swung to Purdy. 'What happened?' It was not a question, but a command to answer, and his face in the moonlight was aloof.

Harden cut in before Purdy could speak. 'Luke killed two scouts. The Apaches are on top, I don't know how many, but if all of them came after us I'd say thirty or forty.'

Bell was sharp. 'Why wouldn't they all come?'

Harden thought that besides being unpopular because of the lost treasure he had incurred this man's jealousy by helping Carol Mayfield with her son, and to try to keep a gloss of peace between them he made his explanation in patient detail.

'There were too many braves for that to be only a scalp hunting party. I don't know where they came from but I'd think they are part of a larger community, with women and children, hiding out down here for a time, with a rancheria somewhere in the mountains. There was a lot of plunder to be had from the ranch that they would not want to be weighed down with while they chased us. I'd say at least some of them would take the goods back to their encampment. What do you think, Luke?'

154

'I think maybe most of them went back. They've got all the stuff from Yecroa to tote too, because we know they aren't anchored between the pueblo and the ranch. We came through there, and they wouldn't have missed seeing us.'

Bell's intolerance of the Negro even though he might owe him his life was undisguised. 'You seem to know a lot about Indians,' he said, leaving the implication that Purdy was suspect to favor the Apaches.

Purdy's brown eyes were steady on the man but not insolent. 'I learned the hard way,' he said, 'chasing their dust.'

'Never mind.' Harden wanted all the animosities kept as far below the surface as possible so long as they all had to be together for mutual defence. There was something else be wanted to establish quickly. With the southerners knowing so little about Indian fighting he wanted himself and Purdy in the command position, and right now was the time to settle that, while Sands and Bell were too uncertain of the situation to think about decision-making.

He said, 'Purdy has bought us some time. We'd better use it to make plans. First, two men here can hold the valley when the Indians do come down . . .'

Fenner interrupted with a yelp. 'Hold it be damned. Let's keep going.'

Harden told him steadily, 'On what? These

155

horses have been moving hard since yesterday morning. They can't keep it up. They need rest. And the women and the boy need rest. And where do you go? How do you get out of here?'

'North,' Bell said. 'Up the river, the way we came in originally.'

Harden looked at him sharply. 'How long before the Apaches could get in that way?'

Bell thought about that, and sounded unsure. 'Take a white man a week. Indians . . . I don't know.'

Harden relaxed again. 'How far is it to where we can find help?'

Bell looked at Sands, at Fenner, and shrugged. 'One hell of a long way.'

Harden held Fenner's eyes until the man dropped his and turned away, then he went on.

'There's plenty of food here, fruit and game as you probably know better than I. We could live here for months.'

Fenner swung back, his voice quarrelsome. 'Who wants to be trapped in here for months?'

'I didn't say we have to.' Harden was finding it increasingly difficult to keep temper out of his tone. 'We won't have to. An Apache has all the patience there is when he sees what he wants and thinks he can get it without too much cost to himself. But if we can knock enough of them off that trail they'll give up and clear out. They'll try to come down, and keep trying, maybe a dozen times, but sooner or later they're going to run out of food and water up there on top and they'll have to pull back to the mountain.'

While he spoke Harden bent and picked five stiff grass straws, left three long and broke two off short, bunching them in his hand with the visible ends even.

'We'll draw. Whoever gets the short straws will stand the first watch. The rest will move on to the old church. The women and Tommy can hole up in the treasure room. It's dry and even if the Indians break through they might not find the tunnel entrance. I had a lot of trouble locating it and I knew where to look.'

Sands' head came up, shaking from side to side. 'Not me this time around. I can't leave Miss Mayfield now.'

Harden agreed with that, and one hurdle was passed. The foreman was not challenging Dave's authority, was more concerned with comforting the blonde woman who clutched at his shirt with white-knuckled hands.

It puzzled Harden that the brown-haired girl had made no move to go to her sister-in-law, had not even looked toward Ethel in her distress since he had been there. Instead, Carol was watching him, seeming to send a silent message of sympathy, to tell him that she appreciated his taking over.

He held the straws out to Bell first. This was the test to see whether Bell would accept his direction. He was not at all certain, and in fact

Bell hesitated, looking to Carol Mayfield. It seemed to Harden that she nodded, but so lightly that in the uncertain light he was not sure. Whether or not, Bell then reached and drew a straw, and it was short. He would be one of the first guards.

Harden did not trust Fenner. The man could panic at a bad moment. Yet it was too dangerous to offend him by leaving him out of the drawing. Bell might keep him in line, but Harden preferred that either he or Purdy share this first duty and he held his breath as he offered the grasses to Fenner. The big red hand came forward reluctantly, hovered, then made the choice. So Fenner, pushed into this corner, would take the chance. Perhaps pushed into another he would fight. Still Harden was relieved that Fenner's straw was long.

It was Purdy who got the second short straw with a quick, casual pluck and no visible reaction. Harden looked at him for a long moment that asked for understanding, then gave his instructions to Bell. He was sure the rider would balk if he thought the Negro was being put over him.

'Take Purdy up where you were and one of you sleep while the other watches. If the Indians show up let them get close enough so that you can hit as many as possible. I don't think they'll come until there's light enough to see. We'll relieve you in about four hours.'

He waited until Bell jerked his head at Purdy and scrambled up the rock slide and lay down just below the crown, seeing Purdy choose a spot some distance away from the southerner. Then he helped Carol to her saddle, put Tommy aboard a horse alone to encourage his young pride, and with Fenner behind him and Sands riding beside Ethel, now wrapped in a tight-lipped remoteness, he headed for the river crossing and the church.

It was still dark when they reached the ruin. They picketed the horses under the trees, then Harden built a fire close to the old orchard. Both Fenner and Sands protested that but Harden lit it, saying, 'They know we're here, and we need light to find something to eat. Go get some fruit for yourselves and Miss Mayfield.'

Tommy and his mother sank to the ground beside the fire, the woman with a half smile, apologetic, saying that she was too tired to eat, but Harden went through the rank growth of the fruit trees, found a banana palm, climbed it and cut a stalk of the fat, stubby, red variety and brought it back. He peeled one and handed it to the boy who ate it mechanically, so sleepy that he hardly knew what he did, and after a moment Carol accepted the one Harden pressed on her.

Ethel sat on her saddle on the ground, removed out of the firelit circle, her back to everyone, chose out of the hatful of peaches, oranges and pomegranates that Sands put in her lap and urged on her, and chewed as if she resented even the human need of food.

Harden, eating on the move, gathered up the horse blankets and took them into the thick brush that hid the tunnel entrance, spread them there disturbing the bushes as little as possible, close to the opening. Then he went back to Sands.

'You'd better bed your people down,' he said. 'And get some sleep yourself. We may have a busy time in the morning.'

The foreman did not answer but he pulled Ethel to her feet urging her gently and, with one arm around her, supported her into the thicket. He did not come back.

Harden picked up the boy, gave Carol a hand and took them to the mouth of the pit, telling her on the way, 'If you hear firing go down to the treasure room, but watch out for snakes that may have crawled in there since the hole was left open.'

He found Ethel stretched rigidly on one blanket with Sands close beside her, an arm across her waist, whether to give her warmth, to protect her or what he could not say. He touched the man's back with a toe and finally let roughness come through his voice.

'They're all in your care tonight. Remember what I told you about Apaches.' But for insurance he gave Carol Mayfield his short gun. Then he went back to the fire. Fenner had curled up close to the horses, possibly to be there in case a jungle cat came after them, or possibly to be ready to bolt if there was an attack. Harden would give him the benefit of the doubt, but he would not rely on the man. He sat down beside the fire and pulled off his boots. He was bodily tired and knew he should sleep, but he had more thinking to do first.

He did not know how the river trail exited from the valley. His first view, from on top with Purdy where they had found the mountain sheered off, had showed that the valley narrowed into a gorge at its north end. If the gorge was passable but still narrow enough to be held, or if the trail went up out of it at a steep angle and could be controlled by two men with rifles, it would probably be best as soon as the party was rested to send them out with game and fruit. He and Purdy could keep the Apaches back long enough for the southern men to get the women and the boy over the rim and safely started across the desert hills toward Hermosillo.

He had no idea how far it was or what streams there were but if Mayfield had brought his herd in from the north there had to be water to make the drive possible. He sat on, musing. He was not asleep but his mind had gradually grown blank when sound behind him brought him quickly to his feet, spinning, reaching for his gun.

It was Carol Mayfield coming toward him.

She saw his sudden move and said in a low voice, 'I'm sorry I startled you, that I waked you.'

'It's all right. I wasn't really asleep.'

She shivered and crouched close to the dying fire, holding her hands over it. The wind through the canyon valley was cold. At that altitude it was cold whenever the sun did not strike a spot directly.

'I put my blanket over Tommy. I couldn't sleep anyway, listening to Sands snore and thinking what might happen to us.'

'Nothing is going to happen to us.' He said it quickly, surely, to ease her worry. Maybe it was because the rest of her party so ignored her that a protective interest in this girl had been growing, as little as they had spoken to each other. 'There's plenty of good fruit, more game here than I ever saw anywhere, and a river full of sweet water.'

'And Indians . . .'

He threw fresh wood on to build up the blaze and shrugged. 'Not in the valley. And they can't get in as long as we keep a close watch. Tell me,' he stretched on the ground beside her, supported on his elbows so that he could look up into her face, 'do you remember the trip when your husband brought the cattle to the ranch?'

Her face twisted in a painful grimace. 'Every day, every hour, every mile.'

He could guess without being told what the

162

effort must have been to move ten thousand wild steers across a thousand miles of desert and mountains like these, but his interest at the moment was in the trail itself.

'He surely couldn't have brought them through here. With a ten-foot spread of horns they couldn't have gone up that shelf. Where did he take them?'

There was agony in her voice and she told a longer story than he needed to hear, but he did not interrupt her.

'We started from the east edge of Texas and crossed it all the way, into New Mexico, maybe even into Arizona. Then we turned south at a place called Agua Prieta and followed a stream down to Nacozari. We went east from there and picked up this river, the Yaqui, and came down it. We turned east away from it again about a three-day ride north of this valley and crossed the badlands above us. A very long way.'

'Was there any trouble coming south?'

'Indians once. Bandits after we crossed the border. But we had a lot more men then. Coming down the river they had to swim the herd. And getting them through the badlands a lot of animals were lost because there was no water.'

Harden thought about this rich valley where everything grew so extravagantly and wondered aloud. 'Why did he go over the badlands? Why didn't he make his ranch in here? No way to get the steers in?'

She made an attempt at a smile. 'You're not a cattle man, are you? There isn't enough grass here, nor room for the herd he meant to build. And he dreamed of bringing in a lot of people, covering the whole mountain with ranches.'

'Did he find the place by accident or did he know exactly where he was coming when he started the drive?'

'He knew. When the War was lost he went to Mexico with General Sterling Price. Price was commissioned by Emperor Maximilian to raise a cavalry unit of thirty thousand confederates to replace the French soldiers who were being withdrawn. You see, the way he explained it to me, when Louis Napoleon of France put Maximilian on the Mexican throne he did it to recover on seventy-five-million francs' worth of bonds that had been issued to the Jecker Company, which had been repudiated by Juárez.

'And Napoleon and Maximilian had made a deal with a William Gwin, who'd been the first senator from California, to bring the miners from California and Nevada who sided with the South down here and work the mines in Sonora as a concession. Gwin was going to be Duke of Sonora.

'Then the French changed their minds and Gwin ran back to the States, but Maximilian still wanted Price to bring troops down and go on with the scheme. My husband, the colonel, came as his aide.

'While he was in Mexico City Tom found some old papers and maps about the mysterious Tayopa mines. After Juárez captured and shot Maximilian, Price's chance for a Confederate concession-state died, but the colonel didn't quit. He never knew how to quit.'

Harden could not tell by her tone whether she thought this was a good quality or sheer stubbornness. He knew that both of them should be asleep, resting, but two things were happening at the fire. Stories of mines and mining always held Dave Harden entranced, and if he could catch only half an hour of sleep before dawn, relaxing wholly as he had taught himself to do, it would be enough. And the girl in talking was relaxing, getting away from the fear of Indians, although her eyes, reflecting the flames, were enormously sad. Her tone changed from the matter-of-fact recitation to a haunted sound that made Harden think of the tolling of a funeral bell.

'Tom escaped, slipped out of Mexico City, but instead of heading for the border and home he came into the Sierra Madres. The country was filled with bandits, Indians, deserters from Juárez' army, but he got through and found this valley and the one where the ranch was built. He didn't find the treasure at that time but he was sure it was

165

here, and with that potential and the mountain his big dream caught fire—an independent Confederate state. He was a big man, six and a half feet tall, very strong-willed. He could have made it all true.

'He rode north, blocking out a way to bring cattle down, and came home to get men to join him, to gather a herd to start with. Everything worked the way he wanted it. He built his ranch, and we all spent the years looking for the treasure. And last year he found it. But it was too late for him.'

The picture of him was impressive to Harden, a giant, probably golden-haired like his son and sister, relentless, driving, refusing defeat either at the hands of the Union or the Mexican patriots. He had succeeded in doing what many others had tried at the end of the War and failed at. He had got his foothold in Mexico and with the Tayopa silver he might well have drawn around him enough Confederates to pry Sonora and the bordering provinces away from the weak Mexican government. He had come so near realizing his dream, and was stopped—not by any enemies but by a simple snake. He thought of Ethel, so driven by the same obsession herself.

'His sister,' he said. 'Do you think she could have carried on if the Apaches hadn't struck, if I hadn't blown the treasure to kingdom come?'

There was a silence, then Carol Mayfield said with a slow bitterness that confirmed his suspicions, 'She might have. She had as much drive as Tom. Maybe more. Neither of them considered themselves ordinary people. They felt they were superior. They didn't live by ordinary rules. At times I have felt that Ethel was nearly insane. She has the drive but not the balance Tom had . . .'

As if the flood gates had sprung open she spilled out her story, the fear and hatred of her father, the short happiness, the War years made all but unbearable by her sister-in-law who held her worthless, her helplessness against the colonel's cold, hard dedication to his single goal.

Never before had she had anyone to talk so to, and afterward she cringed in secret shame that she had opened herself to this man she did not know, who must now believe her an utter fool.

## CHAPTER FOURTEEN

A single shot sent echoes riccocheting back and forth like cannonading between the valley walls. It shattered the dawn.

Harden rolled up from where he slept beside the dead fire, running before his feet were fully under him, snagging up his rifle, heading for the horses. He threw the saddle on and flung up, driving his spurs deep, and raced for the gate. He was aware of Fenner, standing sleep-stupified, and heard Sands crashing through the brush. With the echoes he could not tell how many shots had been fired.

From the first gray light on Luke Purdy had lain bare-headed, his eyes just above the crest of the rock barrier sliding from the curve in the trail to the side, and back, so that his focus did not freeze and delay his sight of a first movement. Bell was sleeping and several times he had snored. Purdy had moved closer to him and each time shook the man to silence. Bell snored as he exhaled and Purdy heard the warning intake of breath, glanced toward him, touched him. When he looked back at the trail there was a difference in the contour of the rock at the curve, a lump that had not been there before.

It stayed there for long moments unmoving. Purdy blinked, wondering if he were mistaken, and knew he was not. His rifle was aimed, his finger on the trigger. The lump moved and became a head as an Indian stepped from behind the shelter and stood poised, looking straight toward Purdy. Purdy did not fire. He wanted the Apache to come on, wanted others to follow, wanted as many in sight as would appear before the first one reached the cut. And he wanted Bell awake, adding his gun. He put a hand over the man's mouth and pinched gently and, when Bell opened his eyes, whispered.

'Look alive now.'

Bell slid down a little further from the crest, turned on his stomach and reached for his rifle. As he brought it up to ease it over the top it grated on a rock—a small sound, but too much. Purdy fired. The bullet went through empty space where the Bronco had been. The copper figure had flashed behind the curve. Bell was swearing gutteral curses. Purdy did not bother. He went back to watching, but with this mistake he knew the Indians would not show themselves so plainly again. They would tease, wave a rag, possibly show an arm to try to draw fire that would use up ammunition. But surprise was gone. It was going to be a long day.

He heard a horse splash across the ford and then Dave Harden was riding in, throwing himself off and scrambling up to Purdy's side, inching his rifle forward, his eyes questioning Purdy. Purdy only nodded for him to look across at the trail.

Harden looked, found it empty and arched a brow at Purdy.

'One showed himself.' Purdy's voice was flat. 'I didn't get him.'

'Only one?' Harden did not understand but something in Purdy's face told him this was not the time for more questions. Whatever had happened, not only was the shot wasted when their lead was limited, when there was no more to be had, but the Indians now knew that

169

this post was guarded. Whatever advantage there had been in the opportunity to cut down the number of Apaches hunting them had been lost fruitlessly. And the opportunity would not come again.

It was useless to pursue the thought. Harden changed the subject, asking, 'Did either of you sleep?'

'I did,' Bell said, and there was a touch of defensive challenge in the words.

Sands and Fenner had arrived and sat their horses down below, looking up, puzzled. Harden told Bell, 'Then you stay here another four hours. Fenner will relieve Purdy and I'll send you something to eat.' Purdy slid down without a word and Harden came behind him, ordering Fenner up.

Fenner hung back, not at all eager to climb, and Harden said roughly, 'You're safer up there than anywhere else. Those Apaches can't come down here as long as you watch sharp. We'll all have to take our turn.'

Fenner still did not go and suddenly Sands bellowed at him. 'Get up there, fast,' and when Fenner scrambled away under his foreman's anger Sands growled. 'Put him against a damn Yankee and he'll fight as good as anybody. But Indians . . .' he shook his head, then looked at Purdy. 'How many did you get?'

Purdy's face was blank, his voice empty. 'None. One showed himself. I waked up Bell and he let his gun drag on a rock. That Indian moved faster than light. He was gone before I could squeeze the trigger.'

Sands said a foul word and Harden cut in. 'Never mind. It's no good wasting time on what's done.' He needed something to take their minds off of what the blunder might mean, and he said, 'Purdy, you go on and get some sleep. Sands and I will try to find some meat. Sands, don't waste a bullet on anything smaller than a deer or a *jabalina*. I'd like to hold off and rig some snares but we need food soon and we can make traps later if we have to stay here a while.'

They rode together toward the river crossing. Sands' sleep had cleared away his fright of the day before and he was thinking again.

'Your shovel and pick that we left at the tunnel when we caught you . . . they're still there. We could dig a pit on a deer trail, brush it over . . .'

Purdy said as they put the horses into the shallow water, 'Probably a lot of fish in here, if we could make a hook and line.'

He heard it first, the crashing through the brush under the trees. They hauled up and made a motion toward the noise. Then Carol Mayfield ran to the river edge waving frantically, and they splashed across.

She was talking, gasping for breath, before she came in hearing distance. The first word Harden caught was *gun*. She was repeating herself, almost babbling when they rode around her.

'Ethel . . . she took the gun you gave me . . . she's wild . . . she's hiding in the orchard . . . she says she's going to kill you and the Negro . . . '

She must have run the whole half mile. Her clothes were torn and her hair flying with twigs tangled in it. Harden dropped at her side and caught her as she stumbled and nearly fell.

Sands was as furious as he had been at Fenner, roaring. 'No, she's not. We need everybody who can shoot until we're out of this. I thought I made her understand that last night.'

But Carol was shaking her head, panting. 'I told her too. I told her to listen to you. I tried to get the gun and she hit me with it . . . she hit Tommy, when he tried to help me.'

The boy arrived in a stumbling run. He was not crying but his young face was white and his deep-blue eyes looked black with their dilation as he ran to his mother and leaned against her.

Harden said, 'Thank you. You rest here and we'll take care of it.'

'You can't,' she said. 'She's hidden. She'll shoot you before you can get close to her.'

'I can get to her.' It was Sands. 'The rest of you wait here.'

'No . . . No . . . ' Carol was insistent 'She's out of her mind. I tell you she hit Tommy . . . she'd never have done that if she knew what

172

she was doing.'

Sands paid no more attention to her but rode away toward the orchard. She sank down to her knees and put her arms around her son, buried her face against his shoulder and the boy, still trying to get his breath, stroked her hair with both small hands in the manner of a grown-up protector.

Over them Harden's and Purdy's eyes met and exchanged a message. Harden had heard many stories of lost mines that were said to carry a curse, and he was about ready to believe it of the legendary Tayopa. The thought made his lip curl in a rueful smile, and Purdy shrugged. Nearly hung, attacked by Apaches, and now a wild woman. That was all they needed.

They heard Sands calling Ethel's name patiently, coaxing. Then there was no sound for a while and then a yell of astonishment and pain, and a second shout.

'Harden. Gimme a hand.'

Harden jumped for his horse and followed Purdy, already spurring toward the orchard. As they came near its straggling edge Sands thrashed out of the trees, wrestling the woman ahead of him. He had a half nelson on her right arm, the hand twisted up behind her back, but she was fighting every inch of the way, kicking back at his shins, wrenching her body. Her eyes rolled, spittle foamed at the corner of her mouth and her light hair fell in strands over her face. She was shrieking in bursts of curses.

'Let me go . . . Let go of me, you son of a bitch . . . Let me get those bastards . . . they killed my country . . .'

Sands wrenched her half around and backhanded her across her face, stunning her. He left blood on her cheek, but it was not hers. He put the hand against his mouth and spat out more blood.

'She bit me.' He said it to no one in particular in an unbelieving voice.

Ethel doubled forward in a quick bend, twisting, either to pull free or throw Sands, and he had to take a step to keep his balance, then he yanked her around, grabbed for the free hand that clawed for his eyes.

'Bitch . . . You're gonna get tied upright right now. Somebody bring some rope.'

The only rope in the party had been looped on Purdy's and Harden's saddles when this flight began and was left at the camping place. Purdy rode for it and Harden went to help Sands control the woman. She was shaking her head violently, flinging the long, loose strands of her hair across Sands' face where they stung and blinded the foreman. Harden swept them back and held them behind her head and she twisted to see him. Like her nephew's, her eyes were dilated, the black pupils swollen, leaving only a narrow electric-blue of iris around them, but there was madness not fear in hers.

Yet she recognized Harden and cursed him. The damn Yankee President had sent him to spy. To destroy the ranch. To destroy the treasure. To wipe out the last hope of the Confederacy.

Purdy came back and it took the three of them to get her down onto the grass, Sands hanging onto her hands, Harden fighting to hold her feet, Purdy tying her ankles and bringing the rope up her back to cinch her wrists, then fastening it close around her waist so that when they released her she could not hurt herself with arching convulsions. Still she spat at them and screamed. They did not gag her, afraid that by accident or malevolent intent she would swallow whatever was put into her mouth.

Then they stood back. Sands' solicitude for her was gone. He sucked again at the ragged bite that had neatly torn a circle of flesh out of his hand.

'Man,' he said in angry awe, 'I never saw the like of that before.'

Harden said, 'Where's the gun she had?'

'Back in the bushes under that first quince tree.'

While Purdy went to look for it Sands went on, shaken, bewildered. 'Damn lucky Carol warned us or she'd have got you two for a fact and maybe me to boot. What in hell are we going to do with her?'

'Have to wait and see,' Harden said. 'And

175

think about it. She's all right here for now, so let's get on with what we were starting.'

Carol came up, eyes round on her sister-in-law, wincing at the screams, asking if she could help, and Harden sent her to take fruit to the barricade for Bell.

Purdy called that he had the gun and that he was going to sleep where he was. Sands and Harden would hunt for game, one on either side of the river. Sands chose the far side, possibly to get away from Ethel Mayfield's animal shrieks and howls.

Harden moved down the near bank, thinking about this new problem. He had been turning an idea around in his mind. He thought that, come late evening, while there was still light for a guard on the rock slide to cover him, he could build a high fire outside the cut that would light the shelf trail down which the Apaches might try a night attack. It could be fed from inside through the dark hours because it would blind the Indians beyond it.

Then, after the party was rested, he and Purdy could hold that barricade while the southern men took the women and the boy north up the river. He figured the two of them could keep the Indians out for three days, which would give the others enough start. The next night, with a last fire burning as if this was no different from the previous ones, he and Purdy could slip away. They should have several hours leeway to put themselves miles up river. When the Apaches finally did come into the valley and read the sign they would discover that the bulk of the white people were out of reach, only two riders within any possibility of being overtaken. He thought they would not follow.

The plan could have worked. But with an insane woman on their hands, what now?

Quail scattered off from in front of him. If he dared use ammunition he could bag enough in half an hour to feast them all, and they had eaten nothing but fruit for more than twenty-four hours. It made a frustrating gnawing in his empty stomach. Then Sands' rifle cracked and his satisfied shout came.

'Got her.'

Harden waded the stream that here was chest-deep. He held his gun over his head and felt his way, slipping, but reaching the far side without going under. He called for guidance and Sand's voice led him to where the foreman was kneeling, gutting a fat doe.

Harden helped with skinning it. They severed the head and cut the body across beneath the rib cage, then, each with a half of the animal over their shoulders they took the long walk back to the camp at the old church.

They had been some hours on the hunt. Purdy was awake and at the camp with a fresh collection of fruit. He already had a fire going in anticipation of the meat. He had driven two forked sticks into the ground and had a sharpened spit ready to hang across them. He reached for the big liver that Harden had speared on one sharp hoof.

'I'm hungry enough to eat it raw,' he grinned, and went to work with his knife, cutting slices, piercing them with his spit.

Carol was sitting on the river bank with a crooked pole, a line made of braided horse tail hairs and a hairpin sharpened on a rock for a hook, showing it to Harden with a wry pride in her ingenuity. Tommy was further down the stream solemnly throwing rocks into it.

Harden began to laugh. Death reached for them on the trail, held back only by Bell's and Fenner's watchfulness. An insane woman lay bound, babbling, choking out an occasional parrot screech from a throat hoarse and rasping. Carol fished. The boy was doing exactly what any child would do with rocks and water, and Purdy cut up and cooked meat as unaffectedly as he would prepare food in any normal camp, using the skin side of the hide they had brought along as his table. No matter the stress, habit was stronger as soon as immediate emergency was lifted.

Sands had dropped his half of the deer and gone to check on Ethel. He came back, shaking his head at Harden's question as to how she seemed.

'Just the same but worn out with yelling.'

'Do you think by tomorrow she could be

tied on a horse and moved out? Could you people handle it?'

Sands' attention sharpened. 'Who knows? What's on your mind?'

'I was thinking that maybe you and Bell and Fenner could take the women and ride up canyon by then. How far is it to Nacozari?'

Sands narrowed his eyes. 'Seventy-five, maybe a hundred miles. What about you and the nigra?'

'We'd stay and hold the back trail a few days, then pull out at night.'

The foreman grunted, took a turn around the camp, then spat on the ground. He did not look very much taken with the idea. He even argued against it.

'It's rough going,' he said. 'Lots of places the canyon narrows and you have to go into the stream bed as much as a quarter of a mile at a stretch. The water's fast.'

'You brought the cattle in that way.'

'We were coming downstream. We shoved them in and let them kick for themselves. We lost quite a few. And suppose them Indians are circling around to come in at us from the north. Suppose we run smack into them?'

'That's one reason you should go as soon as possible. I understand they would have to go through badlands for several days before they could get down to the river, and there's no water along there. They'd have to waste at least a day going back to the mesa to fill some horse guts and get food to travel on.' He turned to Carol. 'When you took fruit to Bell did he say whether he'd seen any more sign of Indians there?'

'Yes,' she said. 'I took the fruit up to him and I saw too. A horse put its head out, and they shook something on a stick to try to make the men shoot.'

'So they haven't left yet. I think they won't go until tomorrow at least. They'll make another try tonight where they are. You'd have plenty of time to get past the branch and if you kept in the water along there they couldn't find your tracks.'

Sands was still reluctant. There was something going on in his mind that Harden did not yet understand. Then the man surprised him by using his own earlier argument to Fenner.

'The five of us can keep them out of here at both ends, and they're going to have to go find food and water sooner or later. We can out-wait them as long as we've got lead, and we have enough if we don't use any more on game to pick all forty of them off one at a time. Besides, they couldn't have driven all the cattle off the ranch. And maybe that rock you blew down can be moved and sorted through and that silver recovered.'

'No,' he decided abruptly, 'I ain't going off and leave you here.'

So that was it, Harden saw. Sands was

clinging to the idea that the Tayopa treasure could be retrieved, and he thought Harden was trying to get him out of the country for his own clear shot at it. With irony Harden recognized the fever that treasure generated in men. In its grip such men would not give up the dream. And the bleak hills of the country were littered with their bones.

The only solution left, he thought, was to reverse his plan, leave the southern men here and he and Purdy try to take the women and the boy through to safety. And a mad woman could make that a task indeed.

No one found anything to say then. They ate in silence when Purdy doled the venison liver around and then the roasted strips of haunch. Sands took meat to Ethel, cut it into small bits, stuffed it down her throat and held her mouth closed until she had to swallow.

Tommy Mayfield sat beside his mother chewing the liver ravenously, wrapped in childhood's isolation from the grown-up world. His seven-year-old mind wrestled with its own terrors, the Indians, even if he had not seen them, like nightmare beasts trying to get to him, his aunt acting like nothing he could have imagined, his world upended and its people spilling off. Two ranch riders had been left dead in the yard, and the men remaining here were no comfort to him. Fenner had always acted ugly to him. Ever since his father had died Sands had been harsh and domineering and he was afraid of the big foreman. Bell had done things for him but he resented the way the man infringed on his claim to his mother, as if he wanted to steal her from him.

Tommy moved closer to her and looked at her face. She did not look worried. She was eating slowly but with determination, as though she did not know when there would be food again. Her eyes were on Harden and the black man and he read in them the things he felt about both men. They had been friendly. Better than their help and their smiles was their way of treating him as an adult. When they spoke to him, asked him to do some chore like bringing dry wood for the fire, or asked a question, they talked as if he were an equal, someone whose opinion was worth listening to. Somehow they gave him more confidence. Harden sent a broad wink across to him now and stood up, finished with his meat, and picked an orange from the pile.

'Time for me to relieve Bell,' he said. 'Sands, catch a nap and come take Fenner's place in about four hours.'

Tommy saw the black man get up and go after Harden and felt that some light had gone out of the day even though the sun was almost overhead.

Purdy trailed Harden out of the hearing of the others and stopped him. 'Dave, you think that silver could be dug out again?'

Again Harden wanted to laugh. 'You too

now, huh? Sure it could. With the big machinery they had at the mine where I worked last. But you'd never in the world get it in here.'

Purdy's smile belied any interest in the silver and he said, 'That don't matter, but I've got me an idea. You take the women and the boy and head out of here. I'll stay and help guard the trail.'

'I was figuring on you going with us.'

Purdy looked out at nothing, saying softly, 'I haven't found the man I want yet. I'll hang around here until I see some bare feet.'

Now Harden was angry at Purdy and showed it in his voice. 'Supposing when you do he isn't here? Suppose he's one of those the colonel sent recruiting?'

Purdy took no offense. 'Then I'll just have to keep looking, won't I?'

'You don't make things any easier on a man, do you?' Harden sounded waspish, and walked on to the guard post. He sent Bell back to the camp for rest.

Fenner complained. The Indians made him nervous and Harden had to keep warning him not to shoot when they made some teasing thrust around the curve, as they did throughout the afternoon.

# CHAPTER FIFTEEN

Manah too had a problem. His two scouts had disappeared down the dark trail, then there had been shooting and the screaming of a horse falling. The time it took for that scream to stop told him it was a very long drop to the bottom. The scouts had not come back. So they had fallen into an ambush of the white people. Manah would not be so foolish as to send anyone else until they could see.

They made their dry camp back from the rim, killed a horse, slaked their thirst with its blood and ate, posted a guard at the trail mouth, and slept.

Manah knew that he had lost face before his remaining men. He had sent two to their deaths and now his troop was down to nine including himself and Gian-na-tah and Santo. Santo by rights should be his lieutenant on this foray, but Manah was wary of the old man, jealous and afraid the famous Bronco might challenge his position as leader if he were made second in command. Santo had ridden with Mangas Coloradas. He had hunted white men from one end of Arizona to the other, he had been Manah's partner through the months of skulking on the lonely trail, and they had come out of the red hills together to join Victorio. Santo did not know fear. He said himself at the council fires that he was already dead, and what does a dead man have to fear?

Manah decided that he had been right in choosing Gian-na-tah over Santo because this night his lieutenant was in a position to say that the leader had made a mistake. None of these Broncos would give him unquestioning allegiance; they would not give Victorio himself that. They followed the old chief because of his reputation for success, and they would follow Manah only so long as they believed he could deliver the whites without too much loss. Two could be sacrificed, but no more.

No one in the party had been as far west as the canyon of Tayopa though they had raided through the Sierra for years. But if they were to succeed here they must get down to the canyon floor. There had to be a way. Manah had never seen a place too rugged for an Apache to enter.

So he waited for light. As soon as the east brightened enough to show the ground, Manah prepared to move. This time he took the lead. If he hoped to recover his lost prestige he had to demonstrate to these hard-eyed men that fear was not in him. He walked, led his horse, and with Gian-na-tah and then Santo spaced well behind him, followed by the other six, he started down the shelf.

The canyon was still in deep shadow. He could not see into its depths. No stretch of the trail was straight for more than a couple of hundred feet and there could be an ambush around every bend. He went only as fast as the growing light showed him what was ahead, and at every curve he stopped for a long study of everything in sight.

He passed two turns, feeling very exposed as he went along the ledge between. At the third place where the rock wall jutted out and cut off his view he put his face against the rock and eased his head along it until one eye could look past it. He saw a horse lying stiff in the trail, almost half its body hanging over the sharp edge. He stretched a hand behind him to stop the line and made no other move. His eye looked beyond the dead animal, searching up every inch of the wall, finding the nose with the rock saddle at its top. The shot that killed the horse must have come from there, or from the trail behind the nose.

Manah stayed where he was for a long white, until the light grew enough to show him every detail in sharp outline. He could find no other eye looking back at him. As a sort of luck piece he wore one scalp from Yecroa tied to the thong of his breechclout. He unfastened it, tangled the hair around the end of his gun barrel and edged it slowly into view, watching intently for movement ahead. It drew no fire, even when he shook it. So he had no choice with the men behind looking on. He had to show himself.

He put an arm out first, then when there was no shot he eased his body into the open. Some time after that he breathed. He beckoned for help and when they had shoved the horse over the edge he led the way with more confidence to the nose and stopped there to investigate. He found the new, small slide and the rubble on the trail where a man had come down from the saddle. It was a good place from which to snipe. Why had the man not stayed there? That he had gone told Manah the whites knew of a better place where there was water, to hold off attack. Up on this saddle a man could be thirsted out. So they must all have gone clear to the bottom.

Now Manah had time and light enough to look down over the canyon. The trail had been much used by pack animals long ago. It curved down the sheer rock wall on a narrow shelf that was even undercut at places so that it hung over the void with no support beneath it. And Manah, knowing all of the rough mountains of Arizona and New Mexico, had never seen anything like the abyss that yawned at his feet.

The downward cliff was as sheer as that above. The mile drop made him dizzy. At the bottom were the soft-looking tufts of tree tops clear across the flat floor and through them, close to this wall, a river wound like a wavy hair, making the valley an oasis in the middle of many barren miles. Up the river some way there was a white building still too dim in the early light to see clearly.

The canyon wall acted as a chimney for an updraft and on it came a faint smell of burned wood. There was no smoke, so the fire had gone out, but the odor meant that the people he wanted had camped somewhere down there. The valley was at least half a mile wide. The wall on the far side was just as vertical as the one Manah stood on. He could see no angling line of a shelf like this one over here, and both walls ran north as far as he could see. Perhaps then the people were trapped down there, unable to get out except by this trail. Perhaps as in many river-cut valleys this one narrowed to a gorge with a waterfall to bottle it up.

He looked down the trail, seeing how it slanted, how sections of it were visible, then chopped off, and another section was visible at a lower elevation. Then it finally disappeared entirely before it met the floor.

Now Manah mounted and rode on, guardedly but convinced there was no one left on this waterless shelf whose retreat could be cut off in the next exposed area. He dropped to the lowest place he had seen from above. From that point the floor was still some two hundred feet below the trail and there was another sharp bend. And here he must be as careful as he was in the beginning. An ambush just beyond here would make sense, for the distance was short between where the angles of the trail and the floor would meet.

He stopped his train, got off the horse again, put it behind him, and again edged his eye out from the rock. There was something different ahead this time. It was still nearly dark down here, but the dim shape of a slanting mound where part of the wall had fallen and blocked the trail could be made out. He could see no evidence that the trail detoured around the flank of the mound but there was a blacker vertical trailwide line rising up from the shelf. So a cut had been made through the middle of the mound.

And that was where the whites would set up their defense.

He tried shaking the scalp on his gun again but at the distance, in the dimness, he knew it would not show. So once again he had no choice. With his balance poised to leap back he stepped out from the rock, listening, his breath held so that even that soft rise and fall would not cover the slightest sound. For a long moment there was absolute silence. Then there came a slight scrape, then a shot. But Manah was behind the rock.

Manah now knew everything he could find out about his quarry from this trail. They were camped in the valley. They had not gone out another way. And they had the entrance closed to him. But they would not be denied him.

He left Gian-na-tah and one other brave

with horses to tempt the white men to use up their shells and took the rest of his band back to the top. They made a mid-morning meal. Then Manah gave Santo an order that brought a gleam into the old warrior's eyes and lifted Manah again above the doubt of the Broncos.

He turned away from the campfire and picked this way on foot along the brink of the rim to learn what else he could of the valley from on top. It was hard walking with no trail, with hardly a foot of level ground and a tumble of ridges to cross, but then he came to the deep wedge out of which the rock slide had thundered at some distant time and climbed down the almost to where it sheered off in a straight drop. From there he had a good view across the valley that was now in full light, of the pattern of trees that crowded against the river on both sides except where the bottom of the slide butted into the water. He looked down on the breast of the slide and saw tiny figures moving there, the air so clear that it acted like a magnifying glass. Across by the white building that gleamed among the trees there was smoke now. That was where the camp was. Good. His survey was complete.

He went back to his men. They had skinned the horse killed the night before, killed and skinned others that could be spared now that the chase was over. They had cut the hides into thin strips and were braiding them into one very long lariat. By late afternoon it was finished. Three hundred feet, untanned and stretchy but very strong—strong enough to support twice the weight of the heaviest man among them.

For the second time Manah led his people down the shelf trail and as the light began to fail they reached the uphill side of the curve where Gian-na-tah and his companion were taking turns teasing the white guards.

He explained to those two who had not heard his plan that Manah and Santo and Gian-na-tah would be lowered onto the canyon floor by the lariat. The boy with his lieutenant was impatient. He wanted to know why all of them didn't go. Manah was pleased with this chance to strut his wisdom.

'Three are enough to do what needs to be done first,' he said. 'We will hide in the trees by the river until dark comes. Then we will cross the river and go around the slide, and when there is moon enough to show us the guards on the back of the rocks we will go up with knives and kill them quietly. Then you can bring the horses and our guns through the cut and we will go to their camp. Here is where it is.'

He squatted to draw a map in the dust. Everyone made sounds of approval that their leader was so thorough, that he planned so well. And even though this was a place of the dead and they must make the raid in darkness, they would all now follow in good faith.

191

With the lariat snubbed around the body of a horse and one man holding the animal's nostrils to keep it from making a noise of protest, Manah put one moccasined foot into the loop fashioned at the end, wrapped the slippery braid once loosely around his forearm and was lowered gently as the rope was paid out. When he was on the ground he freed the rope, yanked on it in a signal and it was pulled up. Gian-na-tah came down next, and then Santo. They concealed themselves and waited for dark.

Just before dark descended they smelled smoke, very close. When it was black enough under the trees that they could not be seen they waded the river and turned toward the slide. They passed the last nose of the curve before the barricade and looked up. Through the foliage they saw the flames of a large fire on the shelf just outside the cut. Manah grunted and tapped the men with him in a gesture of humor. So the white guards wanted light to show them if an Indian came around the bend. They were going to be surprised.

Manah's trio kept going, their feet making no sound on the grass under the trees, until Manah's judgment told him that they had come around the bottom of the slide to the point where its north slope rose back from the river. There they stopped and lay down to wait for the moon.

It would be late reaching all the way down

here, perhaps two o'clock by the white man's count, some seven hours yet. They caught the odor of horses not far off, but the breeze came up from them and Manah thought his Indian smell would not spread against it to reach them and cause them to give a nervous warning.

Some time later he heard an animal splash across shallow water, the jingle of harness, then muted voices. A horse crossed back and went away toward the camp by the building. A guard had been changed, he thought. Supposing that the two extra people in the white party were men, that made a count of five. From his long experience he knew they would take turns watching, probably only two at a time; but if there were three up there, there were three Apaches to climb quietly up behind them and cut their throats before they could make a sound to alert the camp.

He made no attempt to catch the guard who was leaving. There might be a noise made that would spoil his surprise when the moonlight came, and even if there was none he would soon be missed and that too would spoil the plan. Let him go back. Later, when his knives had taken the men on the slope out of their way and the cut was opened for the warriors to ride through, bringing the trio their horses and guns, the sweet smoke of the campfire would guide them straight to the women and whatever men were sleeping there.

Manah was very satisfied.

## CHAPTER SIXTEEN

Luke Purdy waked and looked up at the moon just rising over the canyon's east rim, half an hour high. It already bathed the camp in light enough to show him the cold, cooked venison on the hide, and the fruit. He ate some of the meat, bit into an orange and chewed on it as he mounted and rode quietly out, not waking the others. It was time for him to relieve Sands on the rock slide.

Of the whole party Purdy was least worried about the Indians. He had campaigned against them. He had served beside Apache scouts whom the army hired, and he did not think of the savages as invincible. He knew they were like other men. They made mistakes. They were often at odds with each other in petty jealousies, and they were very cautious when things were not in their favor. The Indians outside this valley knew that the cut was guarded. Harden's idea of building a fire to light that last stretch of trail was a good one. The Apaches would not make any suicidal drive in the face of such odds.

It was dark under the trees and when he reached the river ford the shafting moonlight was just touching the spine of the bare slide. It did not yet show him Bell and Sands up above, lying just under the sharp, angling line of demarcation between light air and dark. Purdy and his horse at the edge of the stream were in the full, soft glow. He got down, tossed the rein loose so the animal could stretch its neck to drink, squatted and scooped a palmful of water into his mouth. Then he called a low hail.

'Purdy here, replacing Sands.'

Sands crabbed down backward until he could rise without his head showing above the mound. Then he stood up, turning.

Purdy was still crouched, drinking.

Gian-na-tah, Always Ready, young and eager, was foolish. The target was too tempting. He came out of the hiding place in a silent rush at Purdy, his knife blade raised overhead ready for a downward thrust into the arched neck.

Manah ground his teeth and Santo let a low growl come up but not pass his lips.

The Indian burst into the moonlight and it flashed from his blade.

Sands saw that and reacted with a yell. 'Behind you . . . Purdy . . .' He did not dare shoot. He did not know which way Purdy would jump. He bounded down the slope and thrashed into the water.

Purdy had lunged forward twisting, throwing his left arm up just as Gian-na-tah jumped him. The knife blow missed his neck and slashed down the forearm, laid the bone bare before Purdy's right hand clamped around the Indian's wrist. With his left arm numbed by shock Purdy wrenched at the Indian, pulled him off balance and they staggered into the stream, but the Apache kept a tight hold on the knife. He twisted away, broke Purdy's grip, and set himself for another lunge.

Then Sands was there, using his rifle in both hands as a club, slamming the barrel against the Indian's head. Gian-na-tah crumpled to his knees, his fingers frozen around the knife hilt, and as he fell the blade sliced down Sands' leg, cutting into the low boot top.

At the sharp pain Sands' finger convulsed on the rifle trigger. The bullet missed Purdy by an inch and killed the horse beyond him. Then, made careless of consequences by surprise and rage, he swung the gun down against Gian-na-tah's back and fired again.

The bloody body sank into the water and slowly turned with the current. Both Purdy and Sands jumped for shore and the shadows under the trees, Purdy drawing his short gun.

If they kept coming in the direction they started they would soon overrun Manah and Santo. The two Indians had only knives and both white men had guns and would now be alert. The Apache smell would give away their position. As if with one mind Manah and Santo made a hurried change in plans. Silently they moved, drifting back over the thick grass in the direction of the camp. The gunfire would probably bring the other white men up here, leaving the women and the boy unattended. This was a chance to take care of them. The valley was big enough to conceal themselves afterward and watch for opportunities to get at the men one at a time. The Broncos still on the trail would have to act on their own and Manah expected that some of them would come down the rope before daylight and join the hunt independently.

Then there were running feet coming toward them and they sank down in the brush. Moonlight made a lace pattern through the branches and through one slender beam a man ran, carrying the boy. A woman passed behind him, then a second man. Manah was disappointed at this, but the second woman was not with these people and so must still be at the camp.

There was another chore for the Indians. If they were not going to be able to get their horses through the cut, then they must put the whites afoot. When the running group was well gone Manah and Santo went on at a jog to find the animals. They were easily discovered, five of them picketed near the camp. Manah would have liked to keep them for his own use, but he could move through the valley more quietly on foot, and if he only took them to another location the whites might find them. So while they neighed and pranced and pulled against the line, frightened by the Indian smell, Santo held the tie lines of one after another and Manah slit the jugular veins.

Then he put his knife back in the sheath at his waist and said, 'Now the woman. If it is the yellow-haired one she is for me. If it is the other, you take her first.' By this generosity he hoped to keep Santo in grateful subordination, because with Gian-na-tah dead Santo was of course lieutenant.

Santo signaled agreement and went looking in one direction while Manah went in the opposite direction. It was Manah who found Ethel Mayfield, lying close by the entrance of the tunnel to the treasure room where Sands had carried her before he went to take his stand at six o'clock the evening before. She had been quieter and Sands had changed her bonds so that she could lie straight.

She had exhausted herself. She had slept, and been waked by gunfire. The wildness in her eyes had changed to the waiting cunning of an animal with one foot caught in the jaws of a trap. She lay in moonlight, her pale hair spreading loose around her head like Medusa's serpents. Manah found her because of the low, rasping voice arguing with itself.

He came silently out of the trees and stood over her. She saw him and her lips pulled back in a feral snarl. He thought it was terror and was pleased. When she made no move to jump and run he thought terror had frozen her. He wanted her to run. He wanted to chase her until she fell and then pounce on her and overwhelm her fighting. That would make his blood race as it should to render all of the satisfaction possible out of her. He made a fierce face, and when she still did not move he reached down and whipped off the blanket that covered her.

He saw the ropes around her wrists and ankles and knew why she had not run. But why was she tied? Might it be that she was a prisoner of the people from the ranch? Were the two extra men in that party possibly outlaws who had raided the ranch before the Apaches overran it? No matter. She was his now, with her slender, trousered body and her soft, white shirt torn half open and her silky hair the color of the sun.

Now Manah defected from his leadership of the warriors. He had what he wanted. The other Broncos did not matter. Santo would understand and take over for the time being. And since he did not choose to be interrupted if the whites came back to their camp, he lifted her, put her over his shoulder and carried her up the canyon—a mile, two miles, three, where her screaming could not be heard no matter how the echoes traveled.

The pop of gunfire reached him but so faint that he knew he had gone far enough, and beyond that he did not wonder who was shooting.

The valley was much narrower here, the floor sloping up gently. The soil was shallower, supporting a lush meadow of grasses but the trees were far apart. In this bright, open space he laid the woman on the ground, on her back, and stood up to rest a little. She was not heavy, but an awkward burden, and he wanted to be at his full strength for the chase. He pulled his knife and cut the rope around her ankles and chafed them to help their circulation because she too should be able to run her best.

He watched her face, ready for any quick move she might make. She did not kick, only looked at him with a fevered brightness in her eyes. She did not seem afraid, and this was something new to Manah. All white women were afraid of Apaches. Again, it did not matter. He took hold of her hair and lifted her to her feet. She did not wince. She found her balance with her feet a little apart, and twisted, asking as plainly as if she used words that her wrists be freed.

Manah was glad to oblige. He cut the binding and dropped it and stood back while she clenched and opened her hands rapidly to restore their use, watching him without expression except for the strange birdlike intensity of her eyes. It would come soon now, as quickly as she felt capable of a dash for escape, and he would let her go a little way before he started after her to make the pursuit a worthwhile game.

Ethel Mayfield felt the tingling grow in her fingers as the blood flowed faster through them. Then it subsided and control came back to her hands. She stood with her head high and shook her long hair back behind her shoulders. Then, as she had done after her idolized brother died, when the foreman Sands had come to tell her that a woman could not manage the ranch, that he was going to assume control, she unfastened the three buttons left on her blouse and spread it wide. Proud of her body, she wore nothing under it. She opened her arms and held them out to Manah.

Manab was rattled. Nothing like this had ever happened to him before. No woman had ever come to him willingly. Yet there she stood, a pale vision, high-breasted, moonlight in the yellow hair. And unafraid. He made a sudden, about-face decision. This one he would not kill. This one he would use carefully. Then he would tie her up again, and when the raiding party was finished and ready to go back to Victorio, Manah would take her with him and keep her. He felt an odd swelling of gratitude to the bountiful gods he had so neglected for so long.

The wild Bronco dropped his knife, dropped his breech-clout and pulled his woman to the ground.

His mouth was on her throat. His body lay on hers. One hand closed on a thick skein of silk-soft golden hair. His other hand went beneath him to rip at her trousers. Heat such as he had never known rushed through him, a terrible, stabbing heat.

His knife blade burned into his side below his rib cage. It was buried to the handle, then pushed down to cut his stomach open and spill its hot coils over the woman's white flesh.

Manah bellowed. He convulsed away. He tried to claw for her neck but his fingers were tangled in the hair and did not tear free fast enough. The woman arched her back with a strong thrust and rolled him onto the ground then rolled herself out of his reach, the knife still in her hand. She got to her feet and watched his pain, his blood and fluids dripping from her fingers and down her legs, until the flopping body lay still. Then she walked down the valley toward the church.

Her mind was a Kaleidoscope of broken pictures. It recognized the valley. It focused on the treasure in the tunnel. It told her to go and make sure it had not been stolen by someone who had no right to it.

## CHAPTER SEVENTEEN

Santo was not often interested in women any longer. He had lived many years and enjoyed many of them in all shades of colors. He had

had a black wife for a time, until she died in a smallpox epidemic. But his time of full virility was passing and now his greater interest was in scalps, in torturing white men and soldiers in particular. He had seen the too impatient boy, Gian-na-tah, attack the big Negro who wore a soldier coat and hat, and Santo had marked that one as his own.

He did not argue with Manah about looking for the woman hidden somewhere around the camp, but neither did he waste his time trying to find her. Manah would do that sooner or later and Santo had no illusion as to what the Bronco would do then. It had been proved to him before that a woman knocked every other thought out of Manah's head. Until he was finished with her he would be no further help to the braves waiting on the trail. Manah was selfish. He would throw away the remaining precious hours of this night when, as the leader designated by Victorio, he should be working to bring the Indians into the valley.

With Gian-na-tah dead and Manah hypnotized by his lust Santo knew that the responsibility for the successful conclusion of this operation fell to him. Saying nothing of this to Manah, and with the killing of most of the white people's horses accomplished, the old warrior quietly went back toward the barricade.

So that they would not by any nervous whinneying give warning that an Indian was near, he kept upwind of the two animals staked out at the edge of the trees by the river for the guards up on the slide. He crept through the dark to where he could see through the brush fringe across the water to the mound of rocks, now in full moonlight.

He located the woman sitting under a big rock at the angle where the slide and the rising wall came together. She had the child in her lap, a boy to judge by the short hair. Her arms were around him and she rocked rhythmically as if she were trying to comfort him.

The tall, heavy man who had rushed into the stream and clubbed Gian-na-tah with the rifle and then shot him in the back sat halfway up the slope, the rifle in his hands trained on Santo's side of the river, stiff and alert. Another man sat hunched, higher up, also with a rifle ready and looking across. His black man and one other lay just under the brow of the slide, their guns pointing up the trail. One man was missing. Santo wished very much that he had a long gun. The targets were very easy. He could kill them all, moving a little after every shot so that his muzzle flashes would draw their aim to the spot he had just left.

He knew where he could get a gun. He could, in fact, signal the braves by jerking on the rope and bring all of them down with guns. They would not need the horses, with all of the whites bunched here in plain sight. All except one, and he wished he knew where that man was.

The whites knew that at least one Indian had come down to the valley floor. The missing man might have gone up along the base of the wall to look for the way Gian-na-tah had gotten in. If he found the dangling rope what would he do then? He would probably go back to tell the others about it, and they would send one or two to make an ambush there to catch anyone climbing up or down. Santo had best get to the rope and get the warriors down before that could happen. Or would he be wiser to make his own ambush and use his knife on any whites who went to the rope? Including himself there were only seven Apaches left functioning, and this procedure should strengthen the odds in their favor against the five white men.

Pondering this question Santo left his watch post and drifted soundlessly back into the trees, then worked parallel to the river. He would go beyond the rope some distance so that in crossing over any accidental splash he might make would not be heard by the alert men on the mound.

*       *       *

Dave Harden heard Sands' two shots when he killed Gian-na-tah and Purdy's horse and knew that there was action of some kind at the barricade. It could be and most likely was the

205

guards shooting at an Indian impatiently showing himself from behind the curve in the trail. But Purdy was up there with the two southerners who were hostile to him even if passively so in the crisis of this siege, and trouble could have broken out between them.

He rolled out of his blanket and sat pulling on his boots. Before he was finished Carol had come to her feet, looking toward the sounds, and Tommy tumbled up beside her.

'Stay here,' Harden said as he got up.

'No.' Her voice was tight with intuition. 'I've got to know what it is.'

Harden did not want to spend time arguing. He swung the boy up in his arms, grabbed his rifle and loped down the path. Carol ran behind him and Fenner, apparently not wanting to be left with no one but Ethel, trailed after her.

They came to the ford and found a golden path of moonlight across it. Harden saw Purdy first, standing in the water holding his left arm with his right. Then he saw Sands sitting on the far bank. He raised his eyes for a quick look up the slide and was relieved to see that Bell at least was in place but turning his head back and forth, watching the trail and also watching Sands. Then he discovered the dead horse lying at the edge of the water and another form caught against it, floating, with long black hair streaming from it.

He put Tommy on his feet in his mother's

care and waded out to the form. Looking down on the body of Gian-na-tah, hanging face down, black blood a dark blot on the copper back, Harden felt his stomach tighten into a knot.

Indians were in the valley.

Where were they at this instant? Holding his rifle ready to use he waded on to Purdy. Purdy's sleeve was shoved up above his elbow and the fingers of his right hand were spread over his forearm, pinching together a deep, long, bleeding gash.

Purdy said, 'You'd better get those people off that bank and up the slide a ways.'

At first Harden did not understand. 'It's wide open over there.'

'But it's out of reach of an Apache with a knife. I don't know how many are in here, but if they'd brought guns we'd all be shot by now.'

Harden waded back quickly, made a fast explanation to Carol and Fenner, picked up the boy and crossed over. Purdy came after them. Sands did not even look up. He was tugging at his left boot, trying to work it off gingerly. Not until he had put the boy down again did Harden see the bloody leg.

'You're cut too? How did they get to you?' Harden could not picture what had happened here.

Then Purdy said, 'I was just coming in, stopped for a drink, and Sands yelled. I'd have been buzzard meat if he hadn't. That Indian was on top of me before I knew he was there. And he might have got me anyway, but Sands came charging over and killed him, got his leg sliced when the Apache fell. How bad is it, man?'

'I don't know yet,' Sands' voice was hoarse with pain. 'Fenner, give me a hand with this boot.'

He leaned back, braced on his elbows and Fenner kneeled at his foot, used his knife to slit the leather boot top further, then peeled it off the foot with a quick jerk, to get it done without dragging out the unavoidable pain.

'Jesus,' Sands gasped. Then, to shove the hurt out of his mind he said, 'I was coming down after Purdy called me. The moon hit that devil's knife or I'd never have seen him. I don't know where the hell he came from.'

While they talked Carol Mayfield had gone to work, pulled the tail of her shirt out of her trousers, borrowed the hunting knife out of Harden's sheath and cut and ripped off strips of cloth. She went over to Purdy, saying, 'Let me see your arm. Did you wash it out?'

He nodded that he had cleaned the wound, warned, 'It's not pretty,' but held the arm toward her, releasing his grip on it.

The edges of the cut spread apart and fresh blood oozed out, but there was no pumping, so an artery was not severed. The girl did not draw back from the ugliness. Squeezing the edges back together as she wrapped, she wound the cloth around the arm as tightly as she could and tied it at the wrist.

'It will stop your circulation,' she said. 'We'll have to loosen it once in a while. Can you move your fingers?'

'Yes. Thank you.' He did, to show her, then they turned to Sands.

Fenner was at the stream washing the foreman's blood-filled boot. Harden had pushed the slashed pants' leg out of the way. The whole side of the hairy leg had been laid open by the knife.

'Work your foot,' Harden told him. 'Let's see if the tendons are cut.'

The man twisted it from side to side, and up and down, grimacing, but proving that the muscles would function. Then Harden eased off the blood-soaked sock and tossed it toward Fenner.

Crouching on the balls of his feet he had turned, had thrown the sock, when the thunderbolt of his glimpse of the foot struck him. For an instant he was frozen. Then deliberately, casually, he stood up and stepped back, trying to put himself between the foot and Luke Purdy, walking toward them. He was too late. Purdy had already stopped, was looking at Sands' left foot. It was missing the two outer toes.

Purdy's dark face was empty of expression, the skin stretched smooth, the mouth closed, firm but not tight. Harden could see nothing about him to show that the big Negro recognized the foreman as Seth Slade, that he was looking at the slave catcher he had come hunting, who had murdered his father and raped his sister and sold her with his mother back into slavery.

Sands' only interest was in his leg, saying, 'Somebody get something and tie this up before I bleed to death. Then let's get the hell out of this canyon before the rest of them Indians come boiling over us. We've got to make a run for it. Now.'

No one answered him. Harden watched Purdy to see what the big, vengeance-driven man would do with his discovery. Would his long-nurtured vision of how he would deal with Slade when he found him explode now and override all other considerations? Would he react involuntarily and kill the man here and now? If his mind kept its control Harden believed that Purdy would not make such a move with a woman and a child looking on. But if the giant rage within him broke loose it would be very bad. He did not dare speak, to remind Purdy that they needed every man, more so than ever now.

The time was not long but it seemed to drag out. Harden thought that Sands, or Slade, must surely wake up to danger in the next instant. Then Purdy turned his back and waded into the river and went to pull his rifle out of the boot on the dry side of the dead horse.

Harden did not treat Sands' leg. A choking revulsion against the foreman made it impossible for him to put his hands on him. He knew Sands was valuable for the gun he could still use, and if by some miracle they could get by the Apaches in the valley only Sands had any chance of controlling the demented woman back by the church. If there was any chance of their escaping north out of here Sands must be kept alive. But Harden could not touch him just now. He walked down to the water and washed the man's blood from his hands.

He was there when Purdy came back and he looked first at the rifle Purdy carried, then into the Negro's face. Purdy showed his teeth in a cold, crooked smile.

'Don't worry so, Dave. I can wait. I'm real used to waiting. Funny though. All along I had my sights set on Fenner. He's more the type. It takes real trash to do what Sands did.'

'Yes,' Harden said. 'Yes. Now I'm going to try to find out how that Apache got down here.'

'You got some kind of an idea?'

'They couldn't have come all the way around through the badlands in this short a time, and this trail is the only other way to get here. But up around that bend it's only a couple-of-hundred-foot drop. If they had some kind of a rope . . .'

211

'Sure.' Purdy sounded disgusted with himself. 'Why didn't I think of that myself! But then where are they? Why haven't they made an attack? They don't have to wait for morning to see us. What do you think it means?'

'I'd say that only two or three came down, with knives, to slip around here and jump the guards without making a noise. Then they could all ride in and surprise the camp.'

'Yeah. That does seem likely. You want me along?'

'No. I may be able to get through alone. Two of us might be easier to spot. You keep an eye on the bottom of the dump in case they try to work around it close to the river . . . or in it.'

'Mr. Harden, sir, I will watch very closely.' Purdy was not being sarcastic, only emphatic.

Dave Harden left his rifle that might reflect light. He carried his short gun in his hand. Before he started he saw that Fenner and Carol Mayfield had bound up Sands' leg, got his boot back on and were tying its split top around his ankle to hold it on. Bell was still on watch at the ridge and Purdy lay down and worked to where he could see over the mound of rock at its lower end.

Harden walked into the river to the middle and turned downstream. He was a fine target for a gun there but he was out of reach of Apaches hidden in the brush if they had only knives. It was not the most comfortable walk he had ever made. At any second if he had guessed wrong a rifle could fire from either shore and finish him. But this was the only possible thing he could think of to do.

He walked with great care, feeling for footing, not committing himself to any step until he was sure a rock would not roll under his foot or his sole slide off a slippery, sunken log. He left the area of the slide and the trees closed down to the bank. Over their tops he had an unobstructed view of the trail lighted by his fire. In the time that had passed since the Apache had jumped Purdy, with everyone's mind pulled away from the fire, the flames had died down to a low glow that did not spread light far. But it told him how far he had come, how far there was to go until he could see around the bend of the wall.

He struck a hole and tried to detour around it, but it stretched to both sides of the stream. He raised his gun above his head and stepped into it. The water rose to his waist, then up his chest, to his chin, and still there was no bottom. He leaned forward, striking out with one arm, swimming, helped by the flowing current. Ten feet later his knee hit against a rock and he nearly went under. He made some splashing in recovering himself, and as the channel bed lifted again he kept down, only his head and gun hand above the surface, half walking or crawling and half swimming. If anyone on the trail looked down he might be mistaken for an otter or some swimming animal.

He reached the place where the channel swept around the curve in an arc that left a small area of flat ground jutting out from the rock, and from there he saw them.

At the distance he made out the bulk of horses lined uptrail and in front of them a tiny fire that glowed red on savage bodies squatted around it. He could not count them but there were nowhere near the number that had hit the ranch. No more than half a dozen here. But that did not mean there were not another half dozen or more around him in the trees. Nevertheless, these Indians were waiting for something and he had more confidence in his first judgment that there were only one or two on the floor of the canyon.

The moon was on the canyon wall and against the slanting lines of the strata he saw the hanging rope, or its shadow, swinging lightly in the updraft.

He had started back upstream, moving with even more care, digging his toes into the bottom and pushing gently forward against the current so that it would not riffle around his neck and throw off sparks of moonlight to betray him, when the new thought all but made him surge to his feet. Where were the other Apaches who had come in with the one now dead? Would they simply have sunk down in the brush and watched the people on the

214

slide in helpless frustration?

No.

He knew where they had gone. He knew Apaches well enough that he should have realized immediately what they would do. They had gone after the horses that were the only means by which the white party could escape. That would be done first, as soon as their surprising the guards had failed. After the horses were gone, probably slaughtered, then those shadow emissaries would return to the rope and call the others down with guns. Then even if some of the white people managed to get away from the exposed rock slide they could be hunted by Indians on foot or Indians mounted, flooding through a cut that could no longer be held.

Time enough had passed by now that they should be coming back any minute—unless they had found Ethel Mayfield trussed up and left all by her insane self at the camp.

Harden had no liking for the blonde woman. In her present state she was one more burden than he needed. But she was a human creature and he hoped they had not found her.

Only one thing could save her and perhaps that was why he had not heard her screams. If she had acted as she had throughout the day, unmistakably crazy, even a Bronco Apache would not lay a hand on her. The superstition of a sort of divinity attributed to the insane was universal among Indians. Harden used the thought as a kind of prayer.

He gave up his slow caution as soon as he was out of the sight line of the Indians on the ledge. His legs churned through the water in long, piston strides. Purdy heard him coming and called sharply but in a low tone.

'What now?'

Harden hit the bank and stalked up it, making a quick, scanning survey to mark where people were. Fenner was up on watch now. Bell had come down to talk to Sands. Sands was on his feet, limping, testing his ability to stand and walk, and Carol Mayfield and Tommy were there watching him. Harden waved Purdy in for a rapid conference. He hated to say what he had to in front of the girl and the child but there was no time left for any subterfuge that would get them out of hearing, and trying to get his breath as he talked he told them what he had seen and what he suspected.

When he mentioned Indians at the camp by the church Carol clapped ber hand against her mouth and gasped. 'Oh, my God . . . Ethel . . . '

Harden took the moment to try to reassure her that an Indian would not harm an insane person, knew that he made little impression but could not afford more time to pursue the issue. Every second was precious now.

'Purdy,' he said, 'can you handle a rifle with one hand all right?'

The Negro looked grimly amused. 'Sure. Why not?'

'I've got to make a try. Now. It's the last chance we'll have. You and Bell get up on top and cover me. Those Apaches on the trail are waiting for a signal to move. They're not watching down this way and it won't occur to them that we'd be rash enough to go up there.

'I'm going up. If I can get to that bend without them seeing me I can step around it and cut down on them. With luck I can get them all, but even if I miss a couple we'll have a better chance to slip away.'

Luke Purdy's face gleamed with a real smile and he glanced at the brown-haired girl. 'Let me go, Dave.'

With that single swift look at Carol Mayfield, Harden knew that Purdy was aware of what had been growing in Harden ever since she opened herself and her vast loneliness to him. He, Harden, wanted to be the one to relieve it. He wanted the girl . . . if they survived.

He shook his head. 'Not with only one good arm, Luke. Don't worry, I'll make it.'

Carol threw out a hand as if she would stop him and a sharp protest broke from her lips. Her eyes were filled with fear for him. He held them with his own, then cut his look away, passed it over Bell and saw the rider's quick pinching-down of his lids. Silently Harden cursed his unguarded moment. On top of everything else he could now look forward to an 'accident' if they did manage to get clear of

217

this valley.

He said with as much calmness as he could call up, 'Luke, give Mrs. Mayfield your short gun. I might need mine up there.' When Purdy passed it to her without speaking Harden told her, 'If it goes wrong, if I don't come back and they break through, do you know what you must do?'

She took the heavy weapon in both hands, folding them around it tightly, and said on a falling sigh, 'Yes.' Then abruptly she turned her back and led her son to the big rock against the wall, sat down and wrapped him in her arms and rocked with him, trying to hold back the keening sounds that crowded in her throat.

Bell was watching Harden with a speculation not successfully hidden. Harden bent to pick up the rifle and said, 'On second thought, you'd better stay here with Sands. Cover this end of the trail in case any Indians get past Purdy and Fenner.'

He did not believe that as insecure as their position was Bell would deliberately put a bullet in his back, but there was a dull, unimaginative quality to the man's mind. If he lay up on the slope with his rifle and his gun sight happened to swing on Harden the temptation might be too great to resist. He was relieved when Bell did not argue. He watched Purdy climb to the ridge and settle himself, then he walked into the cut.

It was only wide enough for a loaded horse or burro to go through, and dark now that the moon, no longer overhead, was moving down the sky. It was all of a hundred feet long and beyond it the fire showed orange. Harden reached the fire reasonably certain that no Indian, if one were watching, could see him until he passed it. After that he would be silhouetted against the flames and he had two hundred feet of exposed shelf to travel. He looked back and up once, but because of the angle he could see nothing of Purdy or Fenner. Then Purdy lifted his bandaged arm in a salute that he was ready and Harden went on.

He had to take two steps through the fire. He crowded against the rock wall and slid one boot under the charred wood there to avoid the crunching noise of stepping on it. He took the second step the same way. The heat of the rock wall scorched through his sleeve as he brushed it and the rock under his feet was hot through his boots. Then he was past it.

He had a strong urge to hurry, to run this gamut before he could be discovered and an alarm could be given, but quiet was too important. He did not look at the curve ahead around which an Apache might peer at any moment. That was Purdy's job. He looked at the path, testing every step to make sure no stone was dislodged to rattle off the edge, and he carried the rifle well away from the wall.

It felt as if it took him a very long time.

219

Every slow step ate into the seconds that were draining away, that might well run out on him before he reached the bend. For all he knew the Indians in the valley might be at the bottom of the rope right now and the ones he stalked sliding down it. For all he knew those in the bottom could be looking up, seeing him. A warning shout could come at any instant.

He still had a hundred feet to go.

Biting down on the impatience that crowded him he moved on, his shadow on the wall going before him, in distracting jerks and darts across the irregularities of the rock. In another fifty feet he had to stop and use his sleeve to wipe away the perspiration that was running down his forehead, beginning to blind him. He dried his palms on his trousers. There must be no slipperiness on the gun when he went around that corner.

He reached it and there had been no shout. He stopped again and drew three deep breaths to steady himself. He stepped around the corner. The yell came up from the riverside then.

There were six Apaches sitting cross-legged around their little fire, playing at some gambling game. The flames threw their hard, sharp faces into strong relief and turned the naked, bronze torsos an angry red. They saw Harden and heard the yell at the same time and sprang apart, diving for the rifles laid nearby.

Harden's Winchester began to fire. He took care to aim before he shot, systematically firing at one and then the next. He knocked down four while they were scrambling for their guns. Another reached his gun on his hands and knees, flung himself around onto his thin buttocks and brought the muzzle up, firing. But he had landed half over the edge. His spasm to try to catch himself spoiled the aim and the bullet went wide. Harden shot him as the spidery figure pitched into space. The sixth Indian was on his feet, stumbling, running toward the horses, a crouched, indistinct target beyond the firelight. Harden fired his last rifle bullet, missed and drew his short gun and shot twice more before the body slumped in a sprawl on the shelf. That was the only body that had not fallen off.

It was over. The sounds of the shots and their echoes slammed against Harden's ears. Then they faded and there was only silence. Harden felt a sagging in his knees and sank down to the trail so that the weakness would not make him stagger to the edge. He sat with his back pressed hard against the wall and waited while a series of reflex shivers shook through him, until his muscles were relaxed, until by testing them he knew they were again under his control. His whole body was wet with sweat and the updraft chilled it. It was a welcome chill.

It was several minutes before Harden could

trust himself to move. Then he gathered up the Indians' guns and one at a time broke them against the edge and dropped them over. He would have liked to take the time to drive the Apaches' horses down to the bottom, but the yell from below meant that at least one Indian was alive and had seen him. From the location of the yell he thought the people at the rock slide could not hear it, so the thing to do immediately was to go and warn them.

\*　　　\*　　　\*

In the valley the Bronco Santo had come around to the river, had looked up in time to see Dave Harden poised to step around the bend, and cried his warning, too late. Then he had stood in frozen horror as the rifle sprayed death, as bodies came hurtling down, crashing through the branches at the bottom of the cliff. He was helpless to do anything from where he was. Only he and Manah were left now of eleven good Apache warriors, and who knew where Manah was. Fury made a fireball inside him. With only his knife for a weapon he was still not going to let these whites go unpunished.

Santo was wily. He had stayed alive a very long time, had been hunted for years. He could still stay alive and with patience, with cunning, he could still take his vengeance. First he must reach and kill the two guards' horses tied near the river ford. Then he would bide his time and watch for his chances.

Santo eased back under the trees and started toward the horses.

*      *      *

At the barricade there was the long, tense waiting for Dave Harden to reappear. Purdy watched the corner like a cat at a mouse hole. Carol Mayfield's eyes were riveted on Purdy for his signal that Harden was coming. Sands and Bell gave all their attention to the lower breast of the mound and the far shore.

When the minutes passed and there was no sign of Harden, Fenner broke. There had been too many shots from the bend. Harden had to be dead. Sands was badly cut and so was the nigger and there were forty red Indians after his scalp. He backed down from the crest, then got up and ran. Purdy knew it and ignored him. So did Carol Mayfield. Fenner floundered across the river toward his horse. As he reached the far bank he heard Sands yell at him but he bolted on. The animal was tied close to the shore. It was stamping, throwing its head, its eyes rolling. Fenner yanked it free, fought it and climbed to the saddle and wheeled to race away.

An Indian was ten feet in front of him, blocking the trail, lunging toward him with a knife.

223

Fenner screamed and wheeled the horse again and dug his spurs deep. The animal sprang toward the river. But Santo reached it in three bounds, caught Fenner's leg and dragged him off. Fenner dropped his rifle and landed hard. Santo was on him like a scrawny panther. The knife blade flashed up and down and drove into Fenner's shoulder.

With the strength born of panic Fenner twisted, caught the Indian's knife hand and threw the Apache away from him. Had Fenner followed up in that second, jumped on Santo while he lay temporarily stunned, he might have made a fight of it, turned the blade on the Indian and killed him. Instead, Fenner wasted his moment scuttling for his rifle. He got it and came to his knees, bringing the barrel around, but Santo was already there in a long spring that knocked Fenner over and the knife drove home to the heart. Fenner fell with Santo on top of him, then the Indian rolled away, dropped the knife and caught up the gun.

In wild, careless triumph, with one white man dead and a rifle in his hands, Santo rose to his knees, weaving his body like a cobra, taking aim up the rock slide. Purdy's shot whistled past his head. Sands shot and missed and killed the horse. Bell waved and shouted at Carol Mayfield to lie down, then joined the firing.

Santo ignored it all. He leveled the sight on

Bell, squeezed the trigger. The bullet went through Bell's face and as he went over backward Santo howled his curdling, ancient war cry and shifted his aim to Sands. Before he could fire again Purdy steadied his rifle on a rock, took deliberate aim and put two bullets into Santo's chest. The blow of the lead made Santo's hand constrict on the trigger. The gun exploded. The bullet whined off rock, hitting no one. Death pulled Santo to his feet, arched him back, slipped the rifle out of his hand and dropped him to the ground.

Carol Mayfield, her attention riveted on Purdy, had not seen Fenner cross the river nor seen the Indian rush on him. Only when the rider screamed did she look across at him and see him pulled out of his saddle by a thing that seemed all arms and legs and flying hair. When the thing came to its knees holding a rifle she knew it was an Apache. She did not hear or need Bell's warning yells. She pushed Tommy flat on the ground and flung herself over him, watching the Indian, holding tight to Purdy's short gun in her right hand.

With her other she stroked the boy's blond hair. He whimpered. She lowered her head to kiss the back of his neck and whisper against it, telling him to lie quiet, that it would be all right. Then she looked up again, listening to the confusing volley of firing, and waited for whatever might happen.

She saw the Indian fall. The shooting

stopped and there was a time of deathly quiet. Gradually, fearfully, unwilling to accept the fact that Bell was dead, that Purdy had not yet made any sign of seeing Dave Harden, had in fact apparently given up watching for him and was now intent on the far side of the river, Carol sat up, hid Purdy's gun in a fold of her skirt and felt its cold, hard message through her hand. It was so long now since she had heard the shooting up the trail. She squeezed all emotion down, all feeling, until there was only emptiness inside her, and forced her brain to take in and freeze on one single thought.

If the Apaches had killed Harden, if there were many of them up there and they now chose to make a suicidal charge, there were only Purdy's gun and Sands' to stop them, and some must surely drive through the cut. She watched its dim mouth, unaware that the increasing light came not from the moon but was the approach of day. If Indians rode in, if they came past Purdy and Sands and on toward her, she must shoot the little boy whom her hand kept pressed down at her side. Then she must shoot herself.

She heard feet running through the cut. Sands heard them and turned his rifle that way, and Purdy brought his attention back from the far shore. A single figure came out, pausing at the mouth for caution, then walking on. It was Dave Harden, alive and apparently not hurt.

His eyes found her and he gave her a quick wave. He looked away to Sands, then up to Purdy and beckoned him down. Carol felt as if she were a stone statue breaking apart when she moved, when she stood up and drew Tommy to his feet and walked toward Harden.

Purdy called ahead on his way down the slide. 'Welcome back, Dave. I didn't see you coming. We were a little busy. What's left up there?'

'Horses. There were only six men. What happened here?'

Purdy looked at Sands, leaving the explanation to him. The foreman's voice was short, embarrassed and angry. 'Fenner. He tried to run out. An Apache stopped him . . . got Bell too before we could hit him. Over there.' He flapped a hand toward the river. 'Harden, are you damn sure there's no more Indians above us?'

Harden did not want to speak to the slave catcher directly. He turned to Carol Mayfield as if the question were hers.

'I'm sure.'

Sands heaved a heavy sigh. 'Then let's go see if Ethel is all right.'

He stood up and limped down toward the shore, the others following. Tommy Mayfield was staring across at the dead Indian in dread fascination, holding tight to his mother's hand. His father's crew had brought him up on harrowing stories of the savages, but he had never seen one this close before, and even lying so quiet the Apache was frightening to look at.

Purdy, close beside Harden, spoke, low, drawling. 'We lost another horse too. That leaves us only one here. Dave, you put Mrs. Mayfield and Tommy on it and take them to the camp, then bring it back so Sands won't have to walk on that hurt leg. I'll stay with him in case there's still an Indian or two around.'

Harden stopped, looking at the one-time sergeant squarely. 'There are maybe a dozen horses up above. I'll go bring them down.'

Purdy moved his head slowly from side to side. 'No, Dave. Apaches have been riding them. They'll be too spooked to be safe for a woman or a wounded man. Do it my way.'

Harden thought that he knew as much about Indians and horses as Purdy did. 'Maybe they'd shy if the Apaches had had them a long time, but these are fat. They're ranch horses.' He started away but Purdy clamped a hand around his wrist and stopped him.

'Dave. Do it my way. This once.'

Looking into Purdy's dark eyes Harden understood. He made no immediate answer. He did not want to lose still another man yet, not until Carol and Tommy were safe beyond doubt But he knew that Purdy's time had come, that he would not wait longer, that Purdy believed there were no more Indians to threaten anyone here. For himself Harden was not that certain. Yet reason told him there could not be more than one, two at most. And Purdy had surely earned the right to make his decision.

'Luck,' he said.

Carol came to return Purdy's short gun. Harden picked up the boy and took Carol across the ford.

He helped them onto the horse and followed it, watchful of the brush around them, listening for a movement among the branches, and listening for a shot from the far shore. It had not come by the time they reached the church and there was no sign of Apaches.

Carol handed the boy down and dropped to the ground saying, 'I'll go see how Ethel is.'

He put a quick hand on her arm. 'Stay here with Tommy. I'll go.'

Her eyes came up and locked on his for a long moment, then she dropped hers and nodded. He went into the thicket around the tunnel entrance where the blonde woman had been left, found the empty blanket and deep moccasin prints of an Indian carrying a burden.

He searched his mind for a way to tell Carol the woman had been taken. There was no easy way. He went back to her and saw that she read his face, and before he could speak she shook her head, indicating the boy. He knew a rush of admiration for her perception and a swelling need to protect her from any further hurt.

He put his short gun in her hand and said, 'I want you and Tommy down in the tunnel now. I'll go first and look for snakes. You wait just inside the entrance and keep a lookout. If anything moves, shoot at it.'

Her mouth tightened, leaving a white line around her lips, and Tommy's eyes were wide, frightened as Harden had seen fear in the eyes of animals. Harden patted his shoulder.

'It's all right, son. Everything's going to be all right.'

Again he picked the boy up, patting his back, holding him tightly to give him a sense of security, but the little body stayed tense.

When Harden put him down beside the tunnel he said in a scared voice, 'Aunt Ethel . . . where is she?'

'Don't worry, we'll find her.' Harden did not know whether his voice fooled the child.

He lit one of the pine torches he and Purdy had used on the day that seemed so long ago and one-handing his rifle went down the steps. It could be that an Apache was in that dark tunnel.

There was no Indian but when he had almost reached the vault a snake buzzed from the room. He stopped, searching the floor in the radius of light and found the coiled rattler in the gloom just beyond, out of striking distance. He hated to use the lead to shoot it, or to make the sound. He extended the barrel of the gun at arm's length, stepped closer. The snake struck at the gun barrel and before it could coil again Harden jumped, came down with his boot on it just behind the ugly head and crushed the skull with the rifle butt. He searched the rest of the room. It was surprising that in the time the tunnel had been left open only the single snake and none of the spiders or lizards of the country had sought this cool haven. He threw the body, still writhing, into an empty chest and went back outside.

'It's clean in there now. I killed one snake. There isn't anything else to hurt you.'

Tommy squared his shoulders defiantly. 'I'm not afraid of snakes. I've killed lots of them.'

'Sure you have.' Harden found a grin of sorts, handed the torch to Carol and told her, 'Take it down and wedge it into the wall of the tunnel where you can see it from the vault, then go on inside and wait. You'll be able to see an Indian before he can reach you if one does come. Keep the gun ready. I'll be back as soon as I can.'

The boy's voice lost some of its new courage. 'Hurry up, will you? I don't like it down there.'

'I know. I won't be long. You take care of your mother.'

He rumpled the boy's hair and went back to the horse. He made a detour to confirm his guess that the animals on the picket line were dead, then rode on toward the rock slide and whatever was to be found there.

## CHAPTER EIGHTEEN

Sands did not object to Harden taking the Mayfield girl and the boy on the horse, but he did not intend to stand here with everybody gone. He did not trust Harden's estimate of how many Apaches might still be in the trees across the water.

'Nigger,' he said, 'get up that trail and bring those horses down. I can knock enough spook out of one of them to get on him and stay on.'

'Let's just wait a few minutes and listen if Dave has any trouble.' The words were quiet, level.

Harden's party had already gone out of sight. Sands turned his head toward the big man up the slope from him.

'Damn you, jump when I tell you to do something.' He had the words out before he noticed that Purdy's rifle was aimed at his middle, and he added, 'And watch where you're pointing that gun.'

Purdy lifted the rifle to his shoulder, his finger on the trigger.

'I know where it's pointing. Just toss yours aside. Your short gun and belt too, Mr. Seth Slade. It's just you and me now. We've got a matter to settle.'

Sands' eyes bugged. He did not know what the nigger meant, but he knew this was not a joke. His rifle was in his hand, its butt resting on the ground. He could neither bring it up nor draw before Purdy could fire.

He said furiously, 'Have you gone crazy? Seth Slade ain't my name. Take that gun off me.'

Purdy's rifle did not waver. His quiet voice did not change. 'I think you are Slade. With two toes gone off your left foot. Now get rid of those guns and walk ten feet away from them. I'm not going to shoot you unless you try to use them.'

Sands was not convinced, but he could not see any choice. He let go of the rifle, unfastened and dropped his belt, saying as he walked the prescribed ten feet, 'All right. Now what the hell is this about?'

Purdy lowered his sight but held the rifle ready. 'It's about a couple of slave catchers who went north to bring runaway folks back south. They weren't too careful about who they took, didn't seem to care whether the black people had free papers or not.'

Sands sucked his breath in loudly and licked his lips that were suddenly dry. 'Somebody else caught you. It wasn't me. I never saw you before you came in here.'

'Not me. Remember back to 59. You and your partner came after a runaway working in a northern shipyard. You found a free black man there too and trailed him to his home. You broke in on him at night, grabbed him and his wife and daughter, loaded them all in your wagon, tied up, and started south. Second night the man broke loose and tried to go for help. One of you shot him down, then you went on with the women. You raped the little girl, one or both of you, and when you got to Mississippi you sold her and her mother as field slaves. That was my family.'

Cold sweat beaded Sands' face. He was more frightened by the calm, deliberate tone than if Purdy were yelling at him. All he could manage was a hoarse whisper.

'I never saw them. I swear it. You ask my partner. He's in Tucson . . . I'll take you to him.'

'I've already found him. He told me you were down here somewhere. He admitted it was you two.'

'Then he was lying. It wasn't me.'

'He didn't lie,' Purdy said. 'A man don't lie while his fingers are being broken one at a time.'

Sands, suddenly desperate, yelled. 'I saved your life just last night. You'd be dead if it wasn't for me and I got slashed up doing it. You can't shoot me in cold blood.'

'Like you shot my father? Like you meant to kill me at the ranch? No, Seth Slade, I can't. I don't want to. I want my hands on you. I do

234

owe you something, and we're pretty well matched now. You with one bad leg, me with one bad arm. It ought to make a fair fight of it, give you that much chance.'

Sands' mind had been scrambling, dredging up ghosts out of the past. The night they had captured the black family and burned their free papers was so long ago. With all that had happened since, he had forgotten. There had been the War, the defeat, the cattle drive down here and the building of the ranch. Then had come the finding of the silver and the colonel's agony of death by snakebite. Everything had gone so well. He was teamed with Ethel and they would control a new country. But then Harden had come, and the Apaches, and now everything was lost except life itself. A moment ago he had thought that too was gone, that he was dead where he stood.

Hope came surging back. He wanted to laugh. He was as big as Purdy, heavier, and he was as good a barroom fighter as the best. He had two hands, the nigger only one, and his hurt leg would not matter when he got the man off his feet.

He watched Purdy take off his belt and throw it aside. Purdy threw the rifle after it and walked toward him. He crouched, his big fingers spread like claws, ready to grapple as soon as Purdy was close enough.

Purdy did not accommodate him. He came in a fast dart and a sidestep. Sands missed his grab and Purdy slashed his right fist into the foreman's face. It shook Sands and he wrenched around, reaching as Purdy went past him. Pain shot up through his leg as though another knife were driven in. It stunned him, straightened him for a flashing moment. Purdy used the time to throw another blow that broke Sands' nose. Sands made a limping lunge but Purdy danced back out of the arms that tried to clench around him, circled him to the place where Sands could not twist to reach him without moving his feet, then put all his weight behind a jab to the side of Sands' stomach. Purdy went on in, driving his shoulder under Sands' arm to knock him off balance.

Instead, Sands hopped on his good foot and this time wrapped his bear hug around Purdy's middle, straining to crush the air out of his lungs, at the same time trying to throw him to the ground where two hands were more important than two legs. Purdy did not fall. His legs were like tree trunks rooted in the rocks. He heaved back, trying to break apart the grip of Sands' hands locked against his spine. Sands hung on, squeezing. Then Purdy brought a knee up hard into the foreman's groin and Sands let go, stumbled and fell.

There was not enough leverage for the knee to paralyze the man but Sands stayed down long enough for Purdy to suck in air to his empty lungs. He stood back, giving Sands time

236

to get to his feet again, ready to go on chopping at him until he knocked him out. Then with his one hand and the strength of the cold rage inside him he would choke the slave catcher to death.

Sands got up. His leg sent pain up to stab through his brain, but he was fighting for his life. He lowered his head, stretched out his hands and drove at Purdy heedless of the blinding pain. Again Purdy dodged aside and as the man charged by crashed his fist against that momentum to the side of Sands' head.

Sands was spun half around. He could not stop. He dove on, falling, his head snapping down on a sharp rock as he landed.

Purdy stood looking at the unmoving man, waiting for him to come up again. When he did not, Purdy went toward him cautiously, expecting a trick, not wanting to be caught again in that crushing embrace. Still Sands did not stir. Purdy stepped in quickly, shoved a toe under him and rolled him onto his back. The bone of Sands' forehead was deeply caved. The man was dead.

The weariness of years flooded through Luke Purdy. He sank to the ground where he was. All strength drained out of him. It was as if only the flame of long-held fury had sustained him to this moment. In this time of body weakness Purdy found that even the fury was purged. Seth Slade was dead, not by Purdy's hand, and that, he found, was good.

He sat empty, and slowly let go of the past. After a while he stood up, went to the stream and hunched down to drink, then to dip water over his face and head. He was there when Dave Harden came back with the horse.

Harden splashed across, looked at Purdy as the big man straightened, then looked up the slope at where Sands lay. He got out of the saddle without speaking. He held no blame against Purdy. If it had been his family Sands had destroyed he too might have tracked the man down and killed him. He walked on to the body, saw the ragged forehead wound and wondered if Purdy had thrown a stone or fought with one in his hand. It did not matter. It was over. Purdy had his vengeance. When Purdy came up Harden did not mention it.

He said, 'An Indian got Ethel Mayfield. Took her off somewhere. Carol and Tommy are down the tunnel. We'd better go back there.'

Purdy did not appear to hear him. His period of emptiness was passing and thoughts were coming in that he needed to talk about.

'I didn't kill him, Dave. I meant to. But I wouldn't shoot him. That seemed too quick, after all the time I looked for him. I meant to beat him, make him hurt, then kill him with my hand.'

'Didn't you?'

'No. I fought him, yes. He rushed me and fell and broke his head.' Purdy rubbed his hand through his hair as though thinking hurt. 'I don't know whether I'd have killed him or not, Dave. Something changed when I saw him lying there, unconscious I figured. He was on his face. It came to me that killing him wouldn't change anything. Revenge wasn't going to make me feel any better about my family.'

Harden felt an unexpected lift of relief. He had come to like this big man more than any other he had known, and he smiled at him.

'Luke, I'm glad for you that it worked out the way it did. You're really a free man now.'

Again Purdy seemed not to be aware that Harden had spoken. He kept on talking as if to himself.

'What makes people act like they do, Dave? Why do they have to hurt each other? Animals don't kill like we do, but only for food or to keep from being food. But men . . . those Indians trying to kill us because the army has been killing them. Who started it all? I just don't understand . . .'

Harden used three fingers to tap Purdy's chest, to call his attention.

'Luke. Listen. We can talk on the way. But there's one Apache still loose around here and Carol and Tommy are alone. Let's go back.'

Purdy appeared to wake up from some disturbing nightmare, but instead of starting for the camp he sank down on the rocky ground, drew up his knees, rested his elbow on one and lowered his face into his hand.

'You go, Dave. I'll be down in a little bit. Right now I can't think good . . . about any more killing . . . even Indians. I've got to have a while to get myself untangled.'

Harden debated. Carol, in the tunnel room with light and a gun, could defend herself against a single Apache and there was only one set of tracks leading away from where Ethel had been. In Purdy's present torment Dave hated to leave him alone here with all the dead around him—Bell and Sands so close, crumpled under the glare of the morning sun, Fenner on the other bank, the Indians over there, the horses, accidental victims of man's carnage.

He sat down a little way from Purdy and to help turn the man's thoughts in another direction said, 'I wonder which is the best way to get out of this country, up the canyon or back over the trail to Chihuahua?'

Purdy lifted his head, looking off to the north as if in his mind he could see the whole valley. A sigh filled his chest and seeped out slowly. He raised his eyebrows, blinking.

'Know something, Dave? This is a mighty pretty place right down here. Plenty of game, lots of fruit, all kinds, all the water and wood anybody'd ever need. And no people to get in trouble with. A man could make a real good life for himself here.'

'You? You thinking of staying? You and I

could do it, but Carol and the boy, they might find it a lonely, empty place to be stuck in.'

The big black man nodded slowly. 'Likely they would. And you . . . you're a prospector. The restlessness would get to you before long. But me, I've always been alone, inside. And I'm real tired of troubles . . .'

His face changed. He was listening, lifting a warning finger.

'Over across, Dave. Somebody's coming.'

## CHAPTER NINETEEN

Carol Mayfield held the burning torch in one hand and the gun hung heavy in her other hand down along her leg. Her eyes followed Harden out of sight as he went back for Sands and the black man, then they were pulled against her will around to the moccasin tracks she had seen going away from Ethel's blanket. Sickness filled her. Tommy tugged at her skirt and sounded anxious.

'We better go down like Dave told us.'

'Yes,' she said. 'We'd best. Go along, I'll bring the light.'

On the way, to keep her thoughts away from Ethel, she asked, 'You like him, don't you, Tommy?'

'Yep. He's better than old Bell, or Sands. When we get someplace else can we go with

Dave instead of Sands?'

'That would be up to Dave, honey, and you mustn't ask him.'

'Why?'

'Because if he didn't want us with him asking would embarrass him.'

'He acts like he likes me . . . and you. Why wouldn't he want us?'

She had always tried to give honest, understandable answers to his questions, and she framed this one carefully.

'Dave is a prospector. That means he goes on trips looking for gold or silver, like he came down here to Tayopa. The country he hunts through is very hard to travel in, sometimes dangerous. We would be a burden to him.'

'No, we wouldn't. I could help look and you could cook for us.'

They were close to the lower room and Carol found a hole chiseled into the wall where other torches had long ago been placed to light the work of priests and Indian bearers as the store of silver was built up. She left the guttering pitch knot there, went on and sat on a box where she could see anyone who came into the area of light. It extended back along the tunnel and forward to cover her and Tommy at its dim edge. She held the gun in her lap, one hand around the barrel, the other around the butt, her forefinger on the trigger. It was heavy for her to lift and she would need both hands to use it.

Now she paid little attention to what Tommy was saying, making up adventures they would share with Dave Harden. She had meant it when she said they would burden a prospector and she had no illusion that Harden would give up that life, but she was glad to have Tommy talking, thinking, not afraid of Indians for a while. She herself was intent on the passage.

They had been there only minutes when the sound came, footsteps grating on the pebbles on the tunnel floor. Carol lifted the muzzle of the gun, resting it on her knee, and held it as steady as she could. Her hands were shaking and she pressed the weapon harder against her leg.

The sounds came closer. Tommy heard them and stopped his words in mid-sentence, swallowing. Something moved beyond the light. Black legs materialized into the glow. Carol fired.

The legs stopped moving, but did not fall. A voice came.

'Who's there? Oh, Carol. What are you shooting at?'

'Ethel.' Carol screamed the name and threw the gun half across the room in front of her in a reflex fear of it.

Ethel walked into the treasure room and the light. Carol choked off another scream at the sight of her, the wild, streaming hair, the open blouse, the awful smears that covered the front of the pants and the dark-stained knife in the hand black to the elbow with drying blood. The face was a quiet mask.

'Oh . . . Oh . . . ' Carol could hardly speak. 'What did they do to you?'

'Who? Nothing.' The light eyes narrowed with suspicion. 'What are you doing here?'

'Hiding from the Indians. How did you get away from them? Are you badly hurt?'

'What Indians? Stop trying to confuse me. I know you came here to steal the silver. I told Tom you would. I came to make sure it was all here.'

'No, Ethel. No, no. You've had a terrible shock and forgotten. Tom is dead. Indians raided the ranch. The silver isn't here. It was blown up with the canyon. Don't you remember any of that?'

A puzzled frown creased the blonde woman's forehead, then she said slowly, 'Oh . . . yes . . . the Yankee spy and the nigra . . . Where are they?'

'They are not spies, Ethel. They are good men. They've been fighting Apaches up at the rock slide.'

'Where are they?'

'Up there now. Sands is hurt and they're bringing him here.'

In a quick, unforeseen stoop Ethel scooped up the gun that lay at her feet and aimed it at Carol. She backed out through the tunnel and at the torch she turned and ran.

Carol knew the one thought that was anchored in that mad mind, to kill Dave Harden and Luke Purdy. Nothing could dislodge it. She came off the box running, chasing her sister-in-law. She caught up with her just outside the tunnel entrance and in a flying dive grabbed the gun, tried to wrench it from Ethel's hand, heedless of the knife the woman still carried.

Brought up short, Ethel spun back and with the force of the spin jerked the gun from Carol's grip, her arm sweeping on to slam the iron barrel against Carol's head. Carol stumbled backward into Tommy as he scrambled out of the tunnel, fell over him and dropped down the steps to the floor ten feet below.

The fall stunned her. She lay only half conscious, Tommy ran down, tugged at her, trying to lift her, crying to her in terror. Her feet were higher than her head, sprawled up the steps. With her senses knocked awry it was a struggle to gather herself, but urgency drove her. She rolled, dragged her knees down and under her, turned, and on hands and feet clawed up the steps, Tommy on her heels. She commanded him to stay there, but he did not obey, too frightened to hear.

Ethel was already out of sight on her murderous mission.

Carol ran after her in the full realization of what would happen if she could not stop the woman. Aside from her personal feeling for Harden, if he and the Negro were killed she had no chance of getting her son out of this country alive.

In her crazy cunning Ethel would hide the gun under her blouse. The men would have no warning. They would be amazed to see her, alive, free. They would look at her clothes and rush to help her, thinking as Carol had that the Indians had spilled her blood in raping her.

Whatever had happened to her it was not that. She would not be able to walk at all, but they would not realize this in time. Ethel would wait until they came so close that she could not miss, then shoot them.

Carol could not wait for Tommy whose short legs could not keep up. He ran as fast as he could but she was outdistancing him. He might have been safe if he had stayed in the tunnel. He might be safe on this trail. But the Indian who had taken Ethel might be near here, might have followed her after she escaped him. She put that thought out of her mind and clung to the possibility that the blood on Ethel was his, that by some miracle she had killed him. It was an evil choice she had to make, to lose precious time by keeping the boy close to her or leave him behind and race to warn the men without whom Tommy would surely die.

In a straight stretch of the path she had a glimpse of the blonde woman far ahead. Ethel was walking. Carol could catch her. Then Ethel looked around, saw her, and ran. She would be across the ford before Carol could reach the river. The trees hid her again as the path made its turn toward the water. In another little time Carol heard the splashing as Ethel ran across the stream and she knew that she could not cry her warning as winded as she was and be heard. Not until she broke out of the trees at the shore where they could see her, would she be of any help. Then she could by wild waving get her message of danger to the men. And she was not there.

\*　　　\*　　　\*

Purdy and Harden, hearing the woman thrash carelessly through the brush, knew no Indian would make such noise. It must, Dave thought, be Carol running for him. She had his short gun and his rifle was in the boot on the horse down at the water's edge. He started for it and Purdy headed for where his guns lay twenty feet away. Then both men stopped as Ethel appeared and rushed into the stream, one hand waving a knife, not in threat but to keep her balance as she waded, the other tucked into her shirt front.

They saw that the shirt was torn open and thought she was clutching it together. They saw the loose, flying hair and the mess of her trousers. Harden had not expected to see her alive again and it flashed through his mind that somehow she had escaped and was now being chased by the captor who had lost her. Both men ran toward her. They were within ten feet of her when she hit the bank and stopped there, panting, out of breath.

The shout came across the river. 'She has a gun . . . to kill you.'

The men hauled up, glancing at Carol stumbling into sight, then at each other and back at Ethel. The woman had the gun out now, aimed at Harden, too steady for comfort, and her lips were drawn back tight against her teeth.

'Talk to her. Keep her attention,' Purdy said.

Harden could think of only one thing that might do that, and he called. 'The treasure. I know a way to get it back. Listen and I'll tell you.'

From the corner of his eye he saw Purdy edge forward. His movement hardly showed, yet he was closer to the woman. Carol splashed into the water to cross. Harden's words had not distracted Ethel, he could almost see her finger tighten on the trigger, but Carol's noise made the woman turn her head. When she turned back both men were rushing on her.

Purdy was a step ahead, lunging between Ethel and Harden. Ethel shot. The heavy bullet went through Purdy's chest, knocked him backward and Harden fell over him.

Dave Harden lay helpless, looking up into the gun barrel and Ethel walked toward him, stalked him, until she was just beyond where he could reach her by any move. It seemed that the gun was almost in his face.

Unconsciously he shut his eyes against the blast. He heard the report. He had no sense of being hit. He opened his eyes. Ethel Mayfield was bent forward at the waist, falling toward him. For a second he did not understand, then beyond the woman he saw Carol, Purdy's rifle banging from her hands, smoke curling out of the lowered barrel.

From the side of his eye he had a glimpse of Tommy, just jumping into the water at the ford. He looked first at Ethel, at the hole where the heavy bullet had broken her spine. Then he dragged himself up and stood over Purdy, knowing that he too was dead. When he turned back to Carol she had not moved. Her eyes were wide on the woman she had shot and hysteria was on its way.

Dave Harden ran for her, caught her shoulders and shook her until her head wagged. She did not react. He took her chin in one hand and slapped her cheeks, one and then the other. He was vaguely aware of Tommy running up, of small fists pounding against his legs, of the boy yelling at him. Carol's mouth stretched wide for a scream and Harden took her head in both hands and clamped his own mouth over hers, holding her face tightly against his. Only when they both had to breathe or burst he lifted his head.

Tommy had stopped beating at him and stood bewildered. The rifle dropped on Harden's feet. The girl shuddered and collapsed against him, rolling her head on his chest as he folded his arms around her and pulled her close. For a while her body was wracked with shaking, then that subsided.

Fresh noises from the entrance to the cut made them swing toward it. Harden stooped for the rifle, but only the horses came through, plodding, heads down, going to the water to drink.

There were no saddles on them. He dismissed them. He left the girl and went to bring up the animal they had been using, to take Carol and her son away from this scene quickly. Carol rode, silent and sagging with exhaustion, Harden carried the boy, and once more they returned to the camp by the church.


## CHAPTER TWENTY

'It's not quite finished yet,' Harden said when he lifted the girl from the horse. 'We can't travel today, start with you two so worn-out. And the Indian who took Ethel from here isn't accounted for. Do you think you can stand another watch in the tunnel while I find him?'

250

He hated to ask it. She had stood up under more than enough and looked near the end of her strength, but he would not dare sleep until be knew the valley was cleared of Apaches. She did not answer him. She picked up a pitch knot and held it while he set it blazing, accepted the gun and followed her boy down the steps, Harden going ahead to make sure the place was still empty.

He left her, mounted the horse and rode down the line of moccasin prints. They were not hard to follow, deep with the weight of two bodies, and at the end of them he found Manah lying as Ethel had left him. He came back and found Santo's tracks leading to the picket line, then going back toward the barricade. That would be the one who had jumped Fenner. He rode on, along the river to the place where the rope still hung, searched the bank and found where three Apaches had crossed, and no sign of more at the bottom of the rope. So that was all. He went back and told the girl.

'I'll get us something to eat,' he said. 'Then you'd better sleep.'

He gathered fruit, shot quail and wrapped them in mud casings and buried them under a fire. But by the time they were cooked Carol and Tommy had eaten bananas and were curled up together under a tree, asleep. Harden ate without appetite, remembering Luke Purdy's enjoyment of the birds the day they found this place. Then he hung his pick and shovel on the horse and went to bury the big black man. He had known Purdy much less than a month, but he felt that he was burying his brother.

At the rock slide he used the horse to drag the southern people and the two Apache bodies into the angle against the wall where he threw down broken rock to cover them all. He could do that much to clean up the entrance to Luke Purdy's luxuriant valley. The horses, the other Indians he left. Animals would eat the carcasses and the bones would return to the soil and, as after the massacre of the *indio* slaves long before, the valley would cleanse itself once more.

He could not lift Purdy to put him over the horse, and finally rigged a travois of tangled branches and towed him to the church. There he made a grave within the walls, roofing it with tiles, and left him in the small encircled grove.

Afterward he bathed in the river, washed his clothes, spread them on bushes to dry and wrapped himself in a blanket. He slept through until the next morning.

When he waked Carol and the boy had roused and built a fire. They ate, a somberness over them keeping them from talking. Then there were decisions to be made.

'We could stay here,' he said. 'We could live here. Go up toward the north end and build a house and live off the land. Would it be too lonely for you?'

Her eyes were still haunted and there was misgiving in them now as she studied him.

Tommy said doubtfully, 'There ain't anything to prospect for here any more.'

That, Harden admitted to himself, was a rub. If they settled here he could not go off and leave these two alone. He would have to give up that whole important part of his life, and it would be a wrench. Yet to have Carol Mayfield it would be worth it. But had Luke Purdy been right when he said that the restlessness would get to him sooner or later?

The girl seemed to read his mind. She said apprehensively, 'If you mean you would want us . . . for a family . . . There is the ranch. The cattle are still there . . . and people will be coming soon. Other families. Maybe Tommy and I could stay with some of them while you were gone.'

Harden was silent, thinking. He had spoken of staying here first because the valley was the most bountiful place he had ever seen. Then with his second thoughts about giving up his old love had come the idea that they could leave Mexico, go back to the States and locate in some town where she would have safe company if his need to look for ore for a spell grew too strong.

Tommy Mayfield, watching Harden closely, thought he saw this man with whom he wanted very much to stay slipping away from him.

'Dave,' he said, 'At the ranch . . . couldn't we prospect for the silver you blew up?'

Dave Harden's first impulse was to smile at the boy's concept. Then he did not. His mind played with the idea. All those tons of rock to move, to sort through with only what machinery he could make in the blacksmith shop. It would take time . . . Years. One man could not do it alone. But there were men coming with cattle and tools, expecting to have the silver to start their new lives with. When they learned what had happened to it, how badly would they want it? Could he make miners out of Confederate ranchers? With a labor force the job might be done.

He began to talk about it. He watched the boy's eyes begin to dance. He looked at Carol and saw that with every word he said the worry in her face relaxed, the haunting shadows faded and a glow of happiness made her beautiful. Harden reached for one of her hands, one of the boy's.

'Son,' he said. 'You've got a deal. Let's you and me go prospecting.' *